Caster & Fleet

THE CASE OF THE CRYSTAL KISSES

PAULA HARMON
LIZ HEDGECOCK

WHITE RHINO BOOKS

Copyright © Paula Harmon and Liz Hedgecock, 2019

All rights reserved. Apart from any use permitted under UK copyright law, no part of this publication may be reproduced, stored in a retrieval system, or transmitted, in any form or by any means, electronic, mechanical, photocopying, recording or otherwise, without the prior written permission of the copyright owners.

This is a work of fiction. Names, characters, businesses, places, events and incidents are either the products of the author's imagination or used in a fictitious manner. Any resemblance to actual persons, living or dead, or actual events is purely coincidental.

ISBN-13: 978-1082834707

For Beatrice Webb
social reformer, economist and co-founder of the London School of Economics

Chapter 1
Connie

It was nap time in the nursery. Bee, who felt herself too grown-up for naps, was at the park with Lily, while George, thumb in mouth and curled in a ball, slept in his bed and little Lydia sprawled in her cot, mouth open and eyes squeezed tight shut.

Nanny Kincaid moved silently about the room, folding towels and putting napkins away in the drawer, with occasional peeks at her charges and the big nursery clock. The hands pointed to a quarter to two. I ought to be in my boudoir completing my toilet, ready to sally forth and pay calls. But five more minutes wouldn't hurt…

I jumped at Johnson's cough. 'Mrs King is on the telephone for you, ma'am.' He looked rather apologetic.

'I'll come at once.' And with one last regretful glance at my currently adorable children, I went downstairs.

'Hullo? Katherine, is that you?'

'I imagine Johnson told you it was,' she replied, sounding amused. 'May I call on you?'

'Weeeeell, it isn't my at-home afternoon, but… Yes, of course you can. Are you all right?'

'Of course I'm all right,' she said, tersely. 'Why wouldn't I be?'

'Oh, no reason,' I said. 'When may I expect you?'

'Say in half an hour?' She paused. 'I've had an odd letter. Well, we have. I'll bring it with me.'

'We?'

'Yes, we. I'll explain when I arrive.' And the call ended.

I regarded the receiver thoughtfully before replacing it in its cradle. Who would write to both of us, and address it to Katherine's house rather than the agency? Admittedly we were both hands-off at the Caster and Fleet agency at present, due to our two comparatively new babies. However, one of us always called in at least once a week to discuss cases with Reg and check anything he was unsure of. Not that there was much of that. I shrugged, and reached for the bell-pull. I would have gone to the kitchen myself; but since we had acquired a few more staff and Mrs Jones had been formally elevated to cook-housekeeper, she was inclined to be territorial.

'Could you ask Mrs Jones to provide a simple afternoon tea for two, please?' I said to Nancy. 'Mrs King is visiting me this afternoon.'

Nancy looked slightly harried. 'Yes, ma'am,' she said, and proceeded down the corridor at a more leisurely pace. I guessed she was not keen to deliver the message. Then again, our under-housemaid Annie would be available to cut bread-and-butter and make tea, so there was no real occasion for injured feelings.

Albert was in the study, sprawled in the armchair with a novel. A brief flurry of arms and legs ensued as he began to right himself; then, seeing it was me, he relaxed. I giggled. 'Lydia takes after you,' I remarked. 'She's all over her cot upstairs.'

'Good girl. But aren't you meant to be getting ready to eat finger sandwiches and make small talk?'

'I've had a reprieve.' He raised his eyebrows. 'Katherine's paying a visit. Apparently she — we — have had an odd letter.'

Albert frowned. 'What sort of odd letter?'

'Oh I don't think it's a *bad* letter,' I said hastily, recalling some of the missives Katherine and I had dealt with on previous cases. 'Katherine sounded keen, not upset at all.'

'Good.' But Albert didn't return to his novel.

'What is it?' I asked.

'Just — look after yourselves.'

'We always do!'

'I mean . . . Lydia's just weaned, and Katherine had a difficult time —'

'Yes, but that was a year ago. It's only a letter.'

'I suppose.' He sighed. 'But be careful.'

***

Katherine arrived even before she had said she would. 'I took a cab,' she said, giving her wrap and hat to Johnson. 'Can we go upstairs?'

'Yes, if you like,' I said. 'Johnson, can you tell Nancy that we shall be in the boudoir?'

'Of course, ma'am.'

'How is Ed?' I asked Katherine, as we went upstairs.

Katherine waited until we were on the landing before answering. 'Hungry. Gwen is shocked at how much he can eat.'

'Surely that's a good thing,' I said.

'I think so. He certainly doesn't take after me.' And Katherine started up the next flight of stairs. I opened the boudoir door, and she sank gratefully into an armchair.

Edwin Roderick James King — Ed for short — had surprised us all by arriving a couple of weeks earlier than expected. Katherine was confined to bed for some time afterwards, and had looked very pale and wan when I had at last been allowed to see her. She had never really spoken about the birth, preferring to concentrate on her baby. Ed had begun life as a long, slim child with a head of dark fuzz and a puzzled expression, as if he were not quite sure where he had found himself, or whether he liked it yet. Now, though, he was a happy soul and filling out nicely — though the same could not be said of Katherine.

She scrabbled in her bag and drew out a plain white envelope, the address handwritten. 'Come and sit by me, Connie, and we can read it together.'

'Who's it from?'

'Come and sit down. We won't be disturbed, shall we?'

'I'm starting to wonder if this is a top-secret mission,' I said, laughing, as I moved a chair closer to hers and poked the fire before taking my seat.

Katherine bit her lip. 'It sort of is. It's from Mr Maynard.'

I stared at her, and then bent over the letter.

Dear Mrs King,

You will note that I have addressed you by your given name and not your professional one. You will also note that I have sent this letter to your home address and not your place of work.

My reason for doing this is that I wish to engage you and Mrs Lamont to undertake an investigation; but no-one must know. I cannot be seen to be committing Departmental funds — or time — to something which most would dismiss as idle curiosity.

For the same reason, I cannot ask you to visit me at the Department, since your presence there during work hours would raise comment and speculation now that your agency is flourishing. Please may I visit you at home on an evening this week, if you and Mrs Lamont are agreeable? If at all possible, I would prefer that no gentlemen of the press were present.

Please could you send your answer to 'Mr Smith', care of Holborn Post Office, to be left until called for.

Yours sincerely,
F.C. Maynard

I looked up at Katherine. 'I see what you mean about "odd",' I said.

'Isn't it,' she muttered. 'He doesn't sound like himself at all.'

I held out my hand for the envelope. 'This isn't franked, it's stamped like an ordinary letter, so it hasn't come through the Department. The postmark is Holborn. He's printed, not written the address. And this isn't Department stationery.' I paused. 'What do you make of it?'

'I'm not sure if he's worried or frightened,' said Katherine. Just then a tap at the door announced Nancy with our tea. 'Ooh good!' she said brightly, stuffing the letter into its envelope. 'Let me tell you what Margaret's been doing.' And she kept up a stream of chatter until Nancy had left the room.

'You didn't need to do that,' I said.

'Mm,' said Katherine. 'If Ada gets an inkling that I'm anything less than bouncing with health, she's quite capable of putting me on bed rest and beef tea.' She laughed; but I sensed that there was some truth behind it.

'Here,' I said, pouring her a cup of tea and handing her a plate. 'A crayfish sandwich or two will keep your strength up.'

'Don't you start,' said Katherine; but she half-filled her plate with good grace.

'What do you want to do?' I said, motioning towards the letter with my egg and cress sandwich.

Katherine chewed, looking thoughtful. 'I think we should receive Mr Maynard's visit, and find out what he actually wants us to investigate. But…'

'But?' From Katherine's frown, it sounded as if it would be a big but.

'If it's something big, I'm not sure we — *I* — can take it on. I mean, there's Ed, and the house to run, and the servants to manage...'

I felt a rush of relief. 'Yes, and I've got Lydia, and George is nearly two, and you remember what Bee was like at that age. And Miss Bee, of course, is far too grown-up to do anything with the babies, as she calls them —'

'Oh good heavens.'

'I know.' I finished my sandwich and brushed the crumbs from my hands. 'Shall we say that if it's something fairly small, where we can delegate most of the legwork to Reg, we'll take it on, but if it seems like a dangling-off-Tower-Bridge sort of case, as your Aunt Penelope would say, we'll decline politely.'

Katherine grinned. 'I'm so glad you agree with me.' She leaned forward and picked up her cup. 'James is speaking at a workers' meeting on Thursday evening,' she said. 'Shall we say then? Six o'clock?'

'Perfect,' I said; although the thought of asking Mrs Jones to move dinner an hour later did not appeal at all. Then a new thought struck me. 'Do you think that James won't approve?'

Katherine's face clouded. 'I *know* that James won't approve,' she said, setting her cup in its saucer with a clack. 'Even if I told him what we'd agreed and how sensible I'm being.'

'Oh dear.' I studied her furrowed brow. 'Are you sure?'

'Oh yes.' She sighed and took a piece of seed-cake. 'Was Albert so protective when you had Bee?'

'I'm not sure. Careful, perhaps.' That seemed the safest answer. But my time with Katherine over the last year had been — different. That was to be expected, I supposed, for a new mother, and I remembered how I had spent most of the first six months of Bee's life in the nursery. Yet we had mostly gone to each other's houses rather than the theatre or music hall. When I had suggested a walk in the park or along the Embankment, Katherine had excused herself on the grounds of the weather, or a later engagement. There had been more afternoon teas, and fewer dinner parties or visits to Simpson's…

I looked up to find Katherine regarding me steadily. 'So shall I write to "Mr Smith" and ask him to visit me on Thursday?'

'Oh yes,' I said, glad to have something else to puzzle over. 'Please do.' I rose and brought my writing case and fountain pen from the bureau.

Katherine pushed her half-finished slice of cake away and dashed off a note. 'That should do,' she said, blotting it and addressing an envelope. 'Thank you, Connie.'

'For what?' I said. 'I can spare you a sheet of paper and an envelope.'

She smiled. 'For not wanting to get caught up in a huge difficult case. I'm enjoying the quiet life.'

I smiled back, and poured us more tea. But even as I did so, I wondered what Thursday might bring.

CHAPTER 2
Katherine

It was good to have the house almost to myself, even if the sound of Ed's wail of 'mamamamama' still echoed in my ears at least ten minutes after Gwen had manhandled him up to bed.

All the same, I felt a little lost with nothing to do. The sitting room sparkled from Susan's hard work, with no trace of the den Ed and I had made earlier. Since I'd given Susan and Tamar an extra half-day off there was no gentle clatter of housework, and without Ed and Gwen, everything seemed unnervingly quiet.

I reread the letter my mother-in-law had sent to James — fussing as ever.

I'm sure you shouldn't allow Ed to walk yet, she'd written. *He's far too delicate. Early babies need a lot of care.*

Ed's as delicate as a steel girder, I thought. *I'll bet a pound to a penny that next time we're at Hazelgrove and Ed is climbing over her like a vine, she'll still be convinced he's not strong.*

I chuckled to myself. *At least without a telephone she can only fuss by letter.*

I half-wished James were there, but he had taken to fussing too and it was rather wearying. Whatever Mr Maynard wanted, Connie and I could consider between us. I glanced at the clock on the mantel. Half past five. Connie would arrive any moment, and Mr Maynard half an hour later. I caught sight of myself in the mirror, wincing a little. My face was too thin, and my dress appeared to have been borrowed from someone much bigger. If Mama was wrong about Ed, she was right about me.

And look after Katherine, she'd added. *She needs feeding up.*

On the mantelpiece was a photograph taken when Ed was a week old. In it I am still in bed, with Ed cuddled against me, and James kneeling by my side. How wan I am in the photograph, and how solemn James appears.

I remembered virtually nothing of the birth or the days immediately afterwards. Just that awful mind-engulfing pain two weeks earlier than I was expecting it, a choking, dragging sensation in my chest and the sickly taste of ether. Only two days before the photograph was taken, I'd come out of a fog to find myself feeding a baby, with Ada fighting off anyone who tried to interfere as if she were a guardian angel with a flaming sword. I almost understood why people kept offering me beef tea, although the next person who offered was likely to have the cup smashed over their head.

The doorbell rang and the sound of Ada galloping to answer came from the hall. Moments later, Connie entered.

***

'What a delightful brood,' said Mr Maynard, looking at a photograph we'd had taken on Ed's first birthday. Ed is sitting close to his hero George, a young man of twenty months. On the other side, Bee holds baby Lydia as if she were a doll. 'Who are they all taking after?'

Connie and I exchanged glances. Bee's independent streak was, I thought, a reflection of her mother's inner fire allowed space to grow, George was calm and measured like his father and Lydia, of course, a little too young to gauge.

'So far, Ed seems more of a detective than a journalist to me,' said Connie. 'Definitely more deeds than words. Has he learnt any new ones this week?'

I giggled. Until recently Ed's vocabulary had consisted solely of names for me, James and Gwen: Mama, Dada and En-en. 'He's just added words for Margaret and Ada,' I said as I poured the tea. 'You'll never guess what they are.'

Mr Maynard grinned. 'Do tell, Mrs King.'

'Maggot and Bissit.'

'Maggot?' exclaimed Connie. 'How did Margaret take that?'

'Fortunately, she thinks it's hilarious.'

'I hope George doesn't copy.'

'She won't mind if he does.'

'Bissit is an unusual way to pronounce Ada, though,' said Mr Maynard.

'Ah, well here she comes and perhaps you'll guess,' I answered. 'It had me and James baffled for a while too.'

Ada entered with a second tray — this one full of savoury and sweet things, including…

'Biscuits!' said Connie.

'Exactly!' I said, 'Ed used to crawl towards the kitchen but we could always catch him. Now he can run and Ada's forever finding him at her side when she's baking. Never, oddly, when she's cooking vegetables.'

'The blessed cherub,' said Ada with a rare smile. 'More people should fill up on sweet things,' she said pointedly as she withdrew. 'Put a bit of flesh on their bones. Do them good.'

Mr Maynard took a biscuit spread with Gentleman's Relish and contemplated it. His face had become solemn and I wondered if he was trying to appear deaf to Ada's inference.

'Sweet things,' he said. 'On the whole, children like them more than adults do.'

Connie contrived to look as if she agreed while popping a petit-four in her mouth.

'As I wrote in my letter, this is not simply a social call,' Mr Maynard continued. 'Delightful as it is to see you both as wives and mothers. Perhaps another time I could meet the, er, "blessed cherubs". I have eight grandchildren of my own. They vary in age. You may think a baby or a toddler is wearying, but the years between fourteen and nineteen are exhausting in another way entirely.'

'We have younger sisters,' I said. 'They're not so far from that age we can't remember.'

'True. True.' Mr Maynard popped a tiny cheese puff in his mouth and took a sip of tea. 'My youngest five grandchildren are aged between three and nine. Quite delightful, all of them, but they have become obsessed with a particular make of sweet. Both my daughters complained separately that the children clamour for Crystal Kisses, especially when they're out and about. Advertising, perhaps? I'm not sure. They're cheap sweets; the nannies and nursemaids can get a great many for a penny. And they would appeal to a small child — bright, colourful...' He withdrew a small paper poke from his pocket and tipped a small pile of sweets onto the marquetry-inlaid table. They looked like marbles or polished gemstones — translucent and brightly-coloured. Every single child would find the reds and yellows and greens infinitely more appealing than the subtle browns and creams of toffees and barley-sugars.

I exchanged glances with Connie again. Had Mr Maynard lost his mind a little? Was he trying to warn us against letting our children eat confectionery?

'I recognise them,' confessed Connie. 'The advertising is colourful and Bee pointed it out. However Nanny Kincaid is very strict about diet, so we've not bought them.'

'I'm not sure I see the appeal myself,' he said. 'Try one if you wish, but they have nothing of the delicacy of Ada's cooking.'

Connie tasted one then pulled a face. 'It's disgustingly sweet,' she said.

'Yes,' said Mr Maynard. 'And although it's usual for

children to like that sort of thing, when offered alternatives — barley-sugars perhaps — they aren't interested. It's just these they crave.'

'I suppose children can become fixated by things,' I suggested, thinking of Ed's small obsessions with specific toys and picture books. 'Thank you for warning us. I'll make sure Gwen knows to take care too.'

'Mmm.' Mr Maynard put his cup down, then sat back with his elbows on the chair arms and fingers steepled. 'You misunderstand, Mrs King. Or at least — I *am* warning you as a friend, colleague and fellow-parent — but as a former employer who thinks highly of your skills, I'm also asking if you and Mrs Lamont would consider investigating these sweets more thoroughly.'

'But why?' said Connie. 'Little shops are full of sweets like these — humbugs, lemon drops, toffees, sold by the quarter-pound for pennies. What's so particular about these ones?'

'They seem to have sprung from nowhere.' Mr Maynard looked at us steadily. 'I'm not sure where they come from and . . . well, my youngest daughter bought some for her children one day to give as a treat later. She said the children were so disagreeable when she said they'd have to wait that she hid the sweets as a punishment.'

'I don't blame her,' said Connie, veteran of numerous battles with strong-willed Bee.

Mr Maynard gave a wry smile. 'Nor I. But little Leo — he's three — managed to find and eat the whole cache in the space of five minutes.'

'Goodness!' I said. 'Was he sick?'

'Worse than that. When discovered, Leo was — well, I've followed your careers, and for ladies of refined and sheltered upbringings you've seen people under the influence of a number of substances in the last five years. Leo was very irritable, tired, and ill with stomach pain for some hours.'

'What on earth caused that?' exclaimed Connie.

'That's the thing,' said Mr Maynard. 'The doctor found nothing to account for it, and sure enough the following day Leo was bright as a button — but desperate — *desperate* for more sweets. Not any sweets, but these. I don't trust them, but I've nothing but a feeling of disquiet to go on so I can't ask for an official investigation. While possibly I could argue my doubts are to do with trade, there's no justification for using departmental resource on what might be a mare's nest.'

'What are they called again?' I asked.

'Crystal Kisses,' said Connie.

'Huh,' said Mr Maynard. 'I call them Crystal Poison. And I think there's something very wrong with them.' He leaned forward and fixed his gaze on us in turn. 'So ladies, will you help?'

CHAPTER 3
Connie

I scrutinised Katherine. Under the polite exterior she looked frankly worried, to someone who knew her as well as I.

'Would you mind if we discussed this alone for a few minutes, Mr Maynard?' I asked.

He raised his eyebrows. 'Of course, if you feel you must.'

'The morning room should be quiet,' muttered Katherine in the hall. 'We'll go there.'

It was quiet; quiet and cold, since the room was never used at this time and the fire was out. 'What do you think?' I asked.

For someone who'd seemed so confident earlier, Katherine appeared overwhelmed; her eyes rested on the window, the door, everywhere but me. 'I don't know,' she said.

'But it isn't anything big, or complicated. Just inquiries at shops, finding out where they get them from, perhaps who their best customers are —'

'I can't spend all day trailing around shops,' she said. 'I just can't.'

'I don't see that we'd need to. Why are you suddenly so reluctant?' I heard my voice rise and took a few deep breaths before speaking again. 'We could ask Reg to do that side of things. All I'd expect us to do is keep a watchful eye in the course of our normal activities; for example, look for any advertisements in the press.'

Katherine's concern was replaced with a small smile. 'I think I could manage that.'

'Then I think we should take this assignment. After all,' I added, more softly, 'if these sweets are aimed at children, and there's anything — not right — about them, then it's in our interest to know.'

'That's true.' Katherine's clasped hands tightened. 'All right then. I agree.'

***

We were about to re-enter the drawing room when the front door opened and James appeared. 'What are you two sneaking around for?' he said, smiling.

'We were discussing whether or not to let Mr Maynard borrow Reg for a little task,' said Katherine.

'Mr Maynard? A little task?' James raised an eyebrow.

'Yes. Reg did work for him, you know. It's hardly unusual.'

'And will you? Let him, I mean?' James's gaze didn't waver from Katherine.

'I don't see why not,' she said, casually. 'Things are quiet at the agency. We'll just let him know.'

James nodded; but I noted that he remained where he was as we went into the drawing room.

'Yes, we agree,' Katherine said — loud enough, perhaps, for James to hear. 'It seems a small task, and easily managed.'

'I hope you're right,' Mr Maynard replied. He stood, and shook both our hands. 'May I ask that you send any correspondence in connection with this matter to the address I gave you?'

'Of course.' I smiled, more to try and lighten the mood than because I felt any pleasure in our agreement. 'We'll do our best.'

His eyes, when they met mine, were serious. 'I know you will.'

***

We apprehended Reg at eleven the next morning in the office, where he was making a fine racket with the typewriter. A brown-paper bag was on the desk beside him, and a bulge showed in his left cheek. 'What are you eating?' I asked, perhaps a little more sternly than I intended.

'Humbug,' said Reg, completely unabashed. 'Want one, Miss F?'

'Perhaps not right now,' I said. 'But it proves you're the man for the job.'

The clatter ceased with one final ping and Reg peered round the typewriter at me. 'What job?'

'We'd like you to investigate some sweets,' said

Katherine.

Reg grinned. 'Well now, you're talking to an expert.'

'Not any sweets,' she said. 'Crystal Kisses.'

'Oh, them,' he said dismissively. 'Now if you'd said pear drops, or something with a bit of go —'

'You don't have to eat them!' I said, laughing.

Reg looked puzzled. 'So what do I have to do with them?'

'Find out who does eat them,' said Katherine. 'We know that children like them, but do adults? And is it just some children? And who makes them?'

Reg whistled. 'Who wants to know, if you don't mind me asking?'

'Our client is called Mr Smith,' I said.

'And I'm the Queen of Sheba,' Reg replied. 'Come off it, Miss F.'

'There's nothing shady about it,' I exclaimed. 'Our client wishes to keep his interest private.'

A sly smile spread over Reg's face. 'You aren't taking bribes from other sweetie manufacturers are you, Miss F?'

'Certainly not.' I drew myself up in my seat. Then the ridiculousness of it struck me, and I giggled. 'If I were, I'd choose a Chocolate Cream.'

'A Chocolate Cream is just a dream,
But who could miss a Crystal Kiss?'

Katherine and I stared at Reg. She recovered first. 'I beg your pardon?'

Reg's face was pink. 'Don't you know it, Miss C? "My Boy Gives Crystal Kisses". It's a music-hall song. I heard it at the Merrymakers.'

'Good heavens, are they even writing songs about the things?' Katherine cried.

'They are, Miss C,' said Reg. 'They're that popular. Thinking about it, the folk at the music hall could probably tell you a thing or two. They know what's in, and what's not.'

'Reg, you're absolutely right,' I said. 'Tomorrow is Saturday. Why don't we go to the matinee and see what we can find out?'

'Could I bring a friend?' Reg asked, his colour deepening.

'If you mean who I think you mean,' I said, 'then she'll be busy with the children, and you will also be at work. And yes, we'll pay your entrance, and you can either have overtime or take a half-day's holiday.'

Reg looked aggrieved for a moment, then brightened. 'I'll start working on the case straightaway, so I can report to you tomorrow.' He paused. 'Could I have money for expenses?'

I laughed. 'Expenses?'

He grinned back. 'Sweets don't buy themselves.'

'Reg, I imagine you're a valued customer at every sweetshop within a mile of here.' I rummaged in my purse and produced a handful of coins.

'Expertise does come at a price,' said Reg, pocketing them. 'Much obliged, Miss F, Miss C. See you tomorrow!' He fetched his cap and coat, and presently we heard his cheery whistle as he thumped down the steps.

'Well,' I said, leaning back in my chair, 'we have begun.'

'Yes,' Katherine replied, glaring at me, '*we* have.'

I sighed. 'What do you mean?'

'What did we agree yesterday? Delegate it to Reg, you said, and we'd just be keeping our eyes open. I don't call dragging ourselves to the music hall and questioning people keeping our eyes open! That's exactly what I didn't want to do!' She got up. 'I'm going home.'

'Katherine, wait. Please.' She looked at me, her hand on the doorknob. 'I don't understand. You love the music hall. It would be fun. We could even take James and Albert, like we used to.'

I had to strain my ears to catch Katherine's next words, she spoke so low. 'It's all right for you, you're not tired all the time.'

I went to her and took her hand. 'Are you?'

She nodded.

'Have you seen your doctor?'

Another nod. 'She said time would probably help. And resting more.' She snorted. 'As if that will happen. Oh, and eating steak and spinach. I'm *sick* of steak and spinach!'

'If your doctor says you should rest more, then you should,' I said firmly. 'I shall go down and get a cab for us, and I want you to rest this afternoon. It's up to you to decide about the music hall. It would be lovely to go out all together, though. Like old times.'

Katherine was quiet in the cab, looking out of the window, and I followed her example. But wherever I saw a shop there were queues, and children with gleeful faces clutching brown-paper bags. Crystal Kisses decorated the omnibuses, and posters twinkled with the gaudy sweets on walls and hoardings.

'Do you see them, too?' I said, turning.

'They're everywhere, aren't they?' Katherine murmured. We were in Bayswater now, and the cab began to slow. She took a breath and squeezed my hand. 'You're right. We must take this on. I can't promise anything, but I'm not so tired I can't try.'

***

I watched Katherine into the house and was pleased to see Ada answer the door. Hopefully she would talk sense into my friend, and not mutter about gallivanting and shenanigans as she usually did when the music hall came up in conversation. I wondered if Katherine would find an excuse not to go.

But why?

How to find out the answer to that question occupied me all the way to Marylebone. There was no point in asking Katherine; whatever it was, she wasn't ready to confide in me. And who else *could* I ask? If Katherine wouldn't confide in me, I was pretty sure that James wouldn't. I sighed, and paid the cabbie.

I was home in time for lunch, and Albert, for a wonder, was home too. I had grown so used to him being at meetings or at Coutts for most of the day that it was a surprise when he came into the dining room.

'Fancy seeing you here,' I said with a smile, as I shook out my napkin.

'Indeed.' He grinned back. 'Once you've served, Johnson, you may stand down.'

'Very good, sir, ma'am,' said Johnson, hastening to the

sideboard.

'I thought you'd be out for lunch,' Albert remarked. 'That's usually what happens when you're at the office.'

'Mm.' I twiddled my fork in my hand, not wishing to say anything until Johnson was safely in the servants' hall.

'What would you like me to do about pudding, sir?' Johnson asked, his spoon poised over a dish of vegetables.

'Don't worry, we'll ring,' said Albert, with a glance at me.

The back of my neck prickled. What did Albert want to talk to me about?

Johnson finally made his exit, and I raised my eyebrows at Albert.

'James telephoned this morning at a quarter-past eleven,' he said. 'He thinks you two are brewing some sort of secret mission.'

'No we're not!' I exclaimed, putting my fork down. 'We've agreed that Reg will do a small piece of work, with minimal input from us.'

'That isn't the impression he got,' Albert said, drily. 'The expression he used was, um, cloak and dagger.'

'Not at all,' I said loftily. 'In fact, I was going to invite you both to accompany us to the music hall tomorrow afternoon, in order to do a little research. It's about sweets.'

'Sweets?' Albert laughed. 'Now that's the sort of case I could be interested in.'

I joined in with the laugh, but not for long. 'Did James sound worried?'

Albert set to work on his chop. 'A bit. Especially when

you picked Katherine up this morning. He's only worried because he doesn't know what's going on.'

'Does Katherine seem different to you?'

Albert's knife paused. 'In what way?'

'Less . . . energetic, I suppose.'

'Ohhh.' The knife began to cut through the meat again. 'Yes. Perhaps she's taking life a bit easier since Ed arrived.'

'I understand that, but when I suggested the music hall she really wasn't keen. You know how she loved it before.' A thought struck me. 'Do you know something I don't?'

'If you mean has James confided in me, no he hasn't.' Albert put down his fork. 'But I'm perfectly happy to come to the music hall with you tomorrow and form my own judgement.' He grinned. 'In fact, as we're both at home you can brief me about our secret mission this afternoon. I wouldn't want to go into the situation without the necessary knowledge.' He cast a glance at the ceiling, and winked at me.

'Oh honestly, Albert.' I couldn't help smiling. But as we ate I wondered what sort of lunch Katherine was having, and whether we would see her, or James, tomorrow.

CHAPTER 4
Katherine

It felt good to be going out unhindered by a perambulator, nursemaid or baby. It was reminiscent of being eighteen and going to my first grown-up dance. I'd been so excited, unable to believe that somehow I was finally allowed. I grinned at myself in the mirror as I straightened my hat, and spun round to hug James.

'Careful,' he chuckled. 'Your hairpins are shooting out like porcupine quills.'

I let him go to check and gave him a thump when I saw he was teasing.

'No more fighting,' he said, pulling me close for a hug. 'And no more secrets.'

I opened my mouth to argue that I hadn't meant to hide anything, but thought better of it. We'd had the whole thing out the previous evening and then made up. Making up had been the best thing. Thinking about it made me grin again.

'Come on,' he said. 'The cab's here. Let's escape before Ed wakes and wants to come too. It's one thing having *you* corrupted by the music hall, quite another for our son.'

'He'd go backstage and work the pulleys,' I answered as we stepped down into the street. 'It could be quite funny. I may suggest it to Mr Templeton as an act.'

James handed me into the cab and settled alongside me. 'You surely don't want to go back on the stage.'

'Not tonight, silly. Although a part of me wonders if I could do it again one day. Unless, of course, we had another baby.'

James took my hand. 'You must build yourself up before we discuss either happening. That's not Mama talking, that's just common sense.'

We fell silent. I knew he was right. I marvelled at how Connie had managed all those masquerade balls when Bee was six months old. When Ed had been that age, I still felt as if I'd been run over by a train. Although perhaps if I'd listened to advice less and gone out more, I might have got my spirit back sooner.

Now, I was torn. I was definitely itching to do something outside the nursery. At the same time, my little boy was growing up and I missed those quiet moments of nursing a baby, with huge trusting eyes locked on mine. Whenever I mentioned it, James would change the subject. He had started writing a novel and doubtless dreaded the crying and restless nights. I wasn't so desperate I minded, but it would have been nice to talk about it properly.

'I've been talking to Mina,' I said. 'She suggests I do

Indian club exercises to build up my muscles.'

'Good grief,' said James, 'I'm not sure I like the sound of that. Either you'd let go at the wrong moment and smash something or Ed would get hold of them and smash us.'

'And I'm out of practice with ju-jitsu too.'

'I can't see how you will need ju-jitsu when you're looking into unwholesome sweets.'

'I won't,' I said. 'That's not what I meant. I could use the Indian clubs to smash the sweets — that's a joke. I told you, Reg is doing all the work, Connie and I are just coming to conclusions. You never used to be so worried about my adventures.'

'I suppose perhaps I think about the consequences more,' said James.

'We're not fools, you know, we've been doing this for six years.'

'I'm not doubting your abilities, just other people's intent.'

'We'll be fine. Let's see what this evening brings and enjoy it. We haven't gone to the music hall for ages.'

James put his arm round me and kissed me softly. 'You're right. Let's enjoy it.'

***

It was no time before we were settled down with Connie and Albert in a box at the Merrymakers. We watched the orchestra tune up and the throng of people milling around below.

'You seem much happier today,' said Connie. 'I was worried about you.' She glanced at James.

'It's his age,' I said. 'He's got over-protective. Or else it's the novel. I think he's stuck. But yes, I'm happier. James and I needed to talk things through. He had the wrong end of the stick entirely. I just want to say —' Connie and I weren't usually sentimental with each other. 'Thank you for your patience with me over the last few months. I'm sorry if I wasn't as patient with you when Bee was small. I'm not sure why I've been so tired.'

'You did all the nursing, remember,' said Connie. 'I had a wet nurse at nights for mine. And they slept through the night early, unlike Ed. You didn't have a decent night's sleep for six or seven months. I bet even now you try to take over from Gwen if he wakes up, and you're still not sleeping properly.'

She knew me far too well. I pulled a face and changed the subject. 'James wants to take me for a weekend at the seaside.'

'Good idea. Someone told me eating seaweed is good for the blood.'

'I'll remember to bring you some back, then.'

'Shh,' said Albert. 'The curtain's coming up.'

With a backdrop of a small town fair, the dancers trooped on stage and started a lively series of country dances while the audience settled. After two tunes, a man in a loud check suit and a bowler hat burst through the middle, flanked by a man dressed as a country bumpkin in a smock costume and straw-covered hat, scattering the dancers and bringing the orchestra to a squeaking halt.

'Nah then, Hayseed,' said Dan Datchett. 'Don't it make you dizzy to watch all this waltzing abaht?'

'Yeah,' said Hayseed, 'but you gotta get used to it. It's the way of the *whirled*. Boom boom.'

The audience groaned.

'What's a townie like you doing out 'ere anyway?' asked Hayseed.

'Fancied a bit o' country air,' said Dan. 'Look at them trees. Talking of trees, why is a dog like a tree?'

'I dunno.'

'Because they both lose their bark once they're dead.'

The cymbal crashed. The audience guffawed and someone woofed.

'How's your wife?' asked Hayseed. 'Bet this fresh air's gingering her up.'

'Not complaining. Tell yer what, I thought of taking her to the seaside next. Only the weather's been that dry I'm wondering if the sea mighta dried up. If it did, what do yer reckon Neptune would say?'

'I haven't *a notion*. Boom boom.'

The audience let out a collective groan.

'So,' said Dan. 'We're going back to the Smoke. There's nothing but turnips out here. I fancy something sweeter. What about you?'

The country fair backdrop rose as the two men went to the side and was replaced by a London street scene showing a pub, a series of shops, a lamp-post and the 'walls' painted with advertising posters. Connie nudged me. Among posters for Bovril, Bird's Custard and Sunlight Soap was a huge one for Crystal Kisses, with a rather nauseating pair of curly-haired moppets opening a paper bag. A glow from it lit their faces.

Ellen Howe stepped onto the stage. She was as dainty as ever despite a cerise dress with exaggerated leg-o-mutton sleeves and skirts just above her sparkling shoes.

She held a paper bag and looked overwhelmed with ecstasy. The orchestra struck up a sentimental tune.

My boy is sweeter than honey
That's supped from sugar cane,
And my heart becomes soft as marshmallow
Whenever he whispers my name.
I melt at his touch like chocolate,
I cannot resist his charms,
His kisses sparkle like sherbet
Whenever I'm in his arms.

No acid drops, no lemon pops,
No sour cherries indeed.
My boy gives Crystal Kisses
And that's all I ever need.
I have a boy whose heart is true,
For a chocolate cream is just a dream
But who could miss a Crystal Kiss?
Only a fool, that's who.

She started to dance, waltzing in the arms of a suave man in tails before stopping to sing again.

How can I ignore his loving
When his gifts are so sweet and bright?
My heart beats to the sound of music

Throughout each wondrous night.
His kisses and caresses enchant me —
I am lost in love, you see.
I feel like a candy princess
Whenever he's here with me.

No acid drops, no lemon pops,
No sour cherries indeed.
My boy gives Crystal Kisses
And that's all I ever need.
I have a boy whose heart is true,
For a chocolate cream is just a dream
But who could miss a Crystal Kiss?
Only a fool, that's who.

'Look.' Connie nudged me. The waitresses passing between the tables were handing out small screws of paper. As we peered over the edge of our box a rap sounded at the door. A waitress came in with a small basket full of brightly-coloured sweets. 'Compliments of Mr Templeton,' she said. 'He says keep 'em for the kiddies if you like. That's what they're best for. Although I give 'em to my old man. Peps him up nicely, it does.' She gave me and Connie a wink and withdrew.

'We must talk to Mr Templeton,' I whispered. I was conscious of James watching us and said more loudly. 'I suppose that was kind of him. I can't speak for you, Connie, but I'm not giving them to either my child *or* my husband.'

'Certainly not,' said Connie. 'It might spoil his

appetite.' Her pause was filled with the noise from the stage, but even in the gloom I could make out a blush spreading across her face. 'I mean later. I mean for dinner. I mean —'

'I'm looking forward to Simpson's too,' I said to rescue her. 'Not beef, though. I refuse to eat beef. If anyone makes me, I swear I shall become a vegetarian. And after that song, I'm not sure about anything too sweet either.'

James chuckled and leaned over the edge of the box as a conjuror came on stage.

'You're right,' said Connie. 'We must talk to Mr Templeton as soon as the show's finished. There's more to this than meets the eye.'

Chapter 5
Connie

Reg arrived at the beginning of the interval ready to burst with news. 'Good afternoon all,' he said, bowing to the box in general.

'Good afternoon, Reg,' said James. 'How goes the mission?'

'It's interestin', that's for sure,' said Reg. 'May I have a word, ladies?'

'Of course,' said Katherine. 'Reg, why don't you accompany us downstairs? I have a fancy to see what people buy.'

James frowned. 'Katherine, have you seen what it's like down there? You'll be pushed and pulled like a sheep at the fair. It makes much more sense for Reg to say whatever he has to say up here.'

It made sense. I couldn't deny it. I looked across at Katherine, who wore a slightly mutinous expression, like a schoolgirl who had been caught out. 'All right,' she said. 'Reg, can you give us the gist of it, and then perhaps we can all go and see.'

She indicated a chair and Reg sat down with a great pulling up of trouser-legs and making himself comfortable. 'I ain't usually in a box,' he said, when he caught my eye. 'I might as well get the most out of it.'

'Shall I go for drinks while Reg gives you the low-down?' asked Albert.

'Oh, would you?' I said, touching his arm.

'Of course. Care to accompany me?' he said to James. 'We can have a quiet pipe without being complained at.'

'I suppose there is that,' said James, getting slowly to his feet. 'Be good, all of you.'

'Now then, Reg,' I said, when the door had closed behind them. 'Spill.'

'Well,' said Reg, leaning in, 'I made the tour of a few sweetshops and grocers of my acquaintance yesterday afternoon. Not just round the office, but on my way home too. And I popped into a few, shall we say, not-so-nice areas while I was about it.'

'And?' Katherine prompted.

'Those blooming Crystal Kisses are everywhere. Every shop has 'em, except when they've run out. In one shop there's even a separate queue for 'em, and the shopgirl was proper put out. "Weigh, tip, weigh, tip, that's all I do all blooming day," she said.'

'Who was in the queue?' I asked.

'No-one older than thirty, I'd say,' said Reg, looking as if that was impossibly old. 'Groups of kiddies, some as young as five, older children with their hems still up, and men an' women of my age and more.'

'How old are you, Reg?' I asked. He raised an eyebrow. 'If you don't mind me asking.'

'Twenty-one next birthday,' he said, looking self-conscious.

'Good heavens. Were they all sorts of people?'

Reg chuckled. 'Yes they were, Miss F. Kids with no proper shoes, clutching a farthing or a ha'penny that they'd got from heaven knows where, and young ladies with frills and parasols, all in the same queue. I ain't never seen anything like it.' He leaned forward still further. 'And here's the thing. I joined a queue and had a listen to what people were saying as they waited. Things like "A bag of these'll keep me dancing all evening", or "These'll give me some get-up-an'-go". The grown-ups, that was.'

'That's probably the sugar,' said Katherine, wrinkling her nose.

'That's what I thought,' said Reg. 'But I tell you what. I, as you know, am a conasewer of sweets, an' I eat a lot of 'em.'

'That is true,' I said, eyeing at his lanky frame and wondering where all that sugar went.

'So I bought a few pennyworths, here an' there, for the purposes of research, and I had a go at 'em. I couldn't eat many, cos they're too sweet even for me, so I had maybe ten. Could I sleep? Could I heck. I was tossing and turning at midnight, and one, and beyond, and my heart was thumping like a drum. Usually I sleep like a log. So something in those sweets keeps you awake and lively.

Something that wasn't there before when I tried 'em, I don't think.'

'*Oh.*' Katherine's eyes were bright. 'If they didn't sound so horrid, I'd get some.'

'I wouldn't, Miss C,' Reg said. 'I woke up with a dry mouth and thirsty as you like. Almost as if I'd drunk too much beer.'

'When you were getting the sweets, Reg,' I said, 'did you happen to see a manufacturer's name on the jar?'

Reg drew himself up. 'I did. Want to guess?'

'No, Reg.' Katherine grinned back. 'I want you to tell me.'

'Fair enough. It was at the bottom of the label, in small type. Fraser's Confectionery.' He looked at us significantly.

'*Fraser's*?' I exclaimed. 'But they're — they're —'

'A well-known firm, founded by Quakers,' supplied Katherine. 'Not as famous as Cadbury or Fry, but established. I thought they made chocolate, not sweets.'

'Well, they're making 'em now,' said Reg. 'And from what I've seen, no other firm is getting a look in.'

The door to the box swung open and Albert manoeuvred round it with a tray of drinks, depositing it on the table. 'Don't know how those waitresses do it,' he said, and handed Katherine and me a small glass of wine each. 'It's heaving down there. I said I'd take the tray as otherwise we wouldn't have got the drinks till the finale.'

'What have you done with James?' I asked.

'He's in the sweet queue,' said Albert, picking up his pint of beer and drinking an inch of it. 'He said he'll be back shortly; he's just observing. I begin to see what you mean about these Crystal Kisses. They're selling bags of them downstairs and the queue is out to the foyer.'

'The power of advertising,' remarked Katherine.

We sipped our drinks contemplatively until a tap at the door announced James. He seemed to have been in a mild altercation; his tie was askew, his collar coming loose on one side. 'I was right not to let you go down,' he said, collapsing into a chair and taking a pull on his pint.

Katherine, eyes flashing, opened her mouth to reply. I nudged her foot with mine, and she gave me an indignant look. 'What happened?' she said, instead.

'It's a bear-pit down there. I joined the sweet queue and within two minutes some glassy-eyed harridan accused me of pushing in, and her young man decided to pick a fight with me. Luckily Ron knows me, or I might have been booted out. But it wasn't just her. People elbowing each other, crowding the counter, snatching the bag from the waitress's hand, offering people in front of them a penny to let them move up. It's — well, not anarchy, but it isn't safe.' He took a long drink of his pint. 'Frankly, you should go and talk to Mr Templeton and see what he thinks he's playing at.'

'What a good idea,' said Katherine, rising. 'We'll do just that.'

***

'You're meant to ask my sekertary for an appointment, you know,' growled Mr Templeton, as we took our seats in front of his desk.

'I do apologise,' said Katherine. 'We forgot the protocol.'

'Yes, you did,' he said sternly, jabbing at us with his cigar. 'Wot you here for this time?'

'We're interested in some sweets. Crystal Kisses,' I said. 'And from what we saw in the first half, you have a special interest in them, too.'

A crafty gleam showed in Mr Templeton's eyes, and he winked. 'Good business, ain't it? And the best of it is, I'm bein' paid.'

'Are you?' I exclaimed. 'Who by?'

Mr Templeton grinned. 'Even I know that ain't good grammar, Miss F. You must be proper rattled.' He puffed on his cigar, blew a smoke ring, then leaned forward confidentially. 'Weeeeell, I had a visit from this commercial traveller, you see. Works for the firm what makes 'em. He made me an offer I couldn't refuse. A nice sentimental song about Crystal Kisses for our Ellen to sing, an' a payment for every night she sings it, *plus* a free supply of the sweeties to give out as tasters. And — *and* — a whopping discount on any Crystal Kisses we buy to sell at the interval. What do you think of that, then?'

Katherine and I exchanged glances. 'It's certainly generous, Mr T,' she said. 'How long has the deal been going for?'

'Two weeks,' said Mr Templeton, crisply. 'And when you add up the payment for Ellen to sing, and the profit we're making on the sweets, it's a good twenty pounds a week extra.' He patted his jacket pocket with a satisfied smile.

'Are any other music halls doing the same, do you know?' I asked, trying to keep my tone one of polite enquiry.

'Probably.' Mr Templeton shrugged. 'If they want to miss out, that's up to them. It's no skin off my nose.' He blew another smoke ring. 'The only down-side, from my point of view, is that me other sales are a bit lacking. Beer an' spirits, an' food too. But the Crystal Kisses make up for that.' He eyed us, and frowned. 'I take it you're looking into 'em.'

'We might be,' said Katherine. 'But if anyone asks, we haven't been in.'

A bell rang — the five-minute warning. 'Awright,' said Mr Templeton. 'But don't you go messing up my business. It's hard enough making a living in this game without a bunch of do-gooding sugar-haters coming down on me. I'd have thought you'd be in favour of less drinking,' he said, censoriously.

'I wouldn't go that far,' I said. 'Do you like the sweets, Mr Templeton?' I gestured at the full bowl on his desk.

'Nah. 'Orrid sweet things. I have 'em for visitors. Now if you don't mind, I've got a show to run.'

***

The dressing room was the usual hive of activity in the last moments before the second half. Performers darted here and there, settling headdresses, tweaking feathers into place, making their smiles bigger, their eyes brighter. One thing, however, was different. A little bowl of bright sweets sat on every surface, twinkling.

'I couldn't manage without 'em,' said Selina, who was now dressed as Madame Cravatini the fake medium. While applying rouge, her other hand grabbed a Crystal Kiss. The sweet twirled between her fingers and she popped it into her mouth. She pushed it into the cheek she had finished rouging, and began painting the other one.

'How many do you think you eat in a night?' Katherine asked.

'Lord, I don't know!' She laughed. 'I ain't buying 'em, am I? I can have as many as I like. And I like the lemon and lime ones best.'

'You can have my share,' said Betty, shoving the bowl towards her. 'Eat 'em till you're sick.'

'Thank you *so* much,' said Selina, and took a green one.

'I'm not so keen either.' One of the younger dancers leaned over for some powder.

'Not refined enough for you, Linnie?' smirked Selina. 'Prefer caviar? You and your posh gentleman friend.'

'Least I got one.'

Selina laughed. 'You won't catch me waiting out in the cold for someone to turn up. Life's too short. Sweets are better'n men anytime.'

'What about you, Ellen?' I asked. 'Do you like them?'

Ellen shook her head. 'They're too much for me,' she said.

'Too sickly?' asked Katherine.

'Not exactly that,' said Ellen, looking thoughtful. 'Too — much. I can't explain it. I don't like the way I feel when I have a few. Like anything could happen.'

'That's what I *like* about 'em!' said Selina, indistinctly. 'I can do the show, an' go for a drink or two afterwards, and dance all night if I want, and then sleep in and do it again.'

'How do you feel in the morning?' Katherine asked.

'Wrecked,' said Selina, with a low laugh. 'But that's staying out all night and overdoing it. Nothing to do with the sweets.'

'No,' said Katherine, her mouth twisting. 'Of course not.'

CHAPTER 6
Katherine

'I'm not sure who'll be worn out first,' said James on Sunday afternoon.

We were following Father and Ed on their third circuit of the park near my family home in Fulham. With his tiny legs, awkward dress and a gait reminiscent of a drunken sailor, Ed still managed to outpace Father despite periodically stopping to examine a blade of grass or piece of gravel.

Thirza, whom my long-widowed father had married nine months earlier, sensibly sat on a bench near the pond, reading a book and minding the pram until it was required. James was right; there was a reasonable chance Father might be the one needing it.

'I'm sorry,' said James, apropos of nothing.

I stared at him. 'Whatever for?'

James puffed on his pipe for a bit. 'I've been fussing

over you instead of supporting you.'

I slowed and pulled him to a stop. 'What brought this on?'

'Albert ticked me off. He said the surest way to make you climb out of a window and go looking for trouble was to treat you like china.'

'Quite right. I owe Albert some chocolates.'

'You do. I saw your eyes light up yesterday afternoon at the Merrymakers in a way I haven't seen for a long time. You sensed a case and you're excited. As I say, I'm sorry. When Ed was born, I started worrying about you and didn't know how to stop. I forgot how capable you are.'

'I've had a baby, James, not a change of personality. Of course I'm capable. All I have to do is use my brain and talk. Plenty of other mothers of babies are doing proper jobs requiring actual muscles.'

'That's not necessarily a good thing,' James said. 'But you're right and I'm sorry. I blame the publisher who's been reading my manuscript.'

'I didn't know it was finished.'

'It isn't, but he's had a look anyway. He says my heroine doesn't cry or faint or rely on the hero enough.'

'Pfft.'

'That's a very ladylike response for you. I really have kept you sheltered for too long.'

I gave him a hard stare and he pulled a puppy-dog face until I laughed. 'If you publish a book with a sentimental heroine, I'll join the Merrymakers.' I said, kissing him and tucking my arm into his. 'James —'

'Yes?'

'I miss the way it was in the beginning, when you, me, Connie and Albert were all in it together. Let's work together on this case like we used to — provided you and Albert don't waste time being knocked on the head or strangled, that is.'

A loud splash a few yards off made us both turn in horror. But Father was the one in the duck-pond, floundering and trying to grab his hat as it floated away.

James rushed over, swept our son up before he could follow into the water and handed him to me so that he could help Father out.

'Papapapa pash!' shouted Ed, straining in my arms. 'Eded pash!'

'No splashing till bath-time,' I said. 'Silly Grandpa.'

'Oh, Roderick,' said Thirza, standing on the edge with her hands on her hips as Father emerged muddy and drenched. 'Whatever did you do that for?'

Ruefully Father stood on the grass and dripped as his trilby slowly sank into the weeds, surrounded by watching ducks as if it were a burial at sea. 'I liked that hat.'

'It was ancient,' said Thirza. 'The ducks are welcome to it. What shall I do with you?'

'Give me a hug?' suggested Father with his arms outstretched. His white hair was plastered flat to his head and his beard draggled.

'Certainly not,' said Thirza, although she giggled and went pink. They were both well into their sixties but you'd never have known by their behaviour. Their autumn romance was the main reason Margaret had moved in with James and me. She considered us, generally speaking, less mortifying.

'Well, then,' said Father with dignity as he squelched up the path. 'I shall have a bath and a cup of cocoa and if I don't get a hug, I'll have some Crystal Kisses instead.'

James and I exchanged glances. 'Have you taken to eating them, Father?' I said with care.

'Not yet,' said Father, shivering. 'But the advertising was splendid and I bought some. Is Ed too young for them?'

'Yes,' I said. 'Far too young. And I'm not sure they're good for you either. I don't think the doctor would be happy about you eating them.'

Father looked a little crestfallen. 'Really? They said they made you work nineteen to the dozen. I have too many ideas and not enough energy.'

'Who's "they", Father?'

'Oh —' Father paused in his stride homewards. 'Someone at one of my lectures, now was it in Kensington or Kendal or Kidderminster or —'

'Stop stopping, Roderick,' urged Thirza.

Father started moving again. 'What a pity. I'll have to try something else. Oh, and by the way,' he added as he squelched up the steps and, to the horror of the maid, across the sparkling tiles in the hall, 'Th-thirza and I are p-planning an adventure abroad later this y-year. Not so far — F-france perhaps. We thought maybe y-y-you th-three could come too. I d-daresay M-margaret will be too busy. Sh-she usually is.'

'Stop dawdling, do,' said Thirza, steering him up the stairs. 'Or you'll catch your death. As for those sweets, I knew they were too gaudy to be good for you. I'll throw them out and get you something healthy like a piece of ginger cake with your cocoa to warm you up.'

'Don't throw the sweets out, Thirza,' I said. 'Please, give them to me. I'll — I'll get rid of them for you.'

***

By the time we'd returned to Bayswater, Margaret was home. James went off to battle with his novel while Gwen took Ed up for his bath.

Margaret was torn between laughing at Father's accident and worrying about his health.

'He seemed well enough,' I reassured her. 'When we left he was warmed through and in his smoking jacket and cap, sitting by the fire with his feet on a hot water bottle and Thirza cuddled up.'

Margaret pulled a revolted face. 'Old people shouldn't be allowed to do that sort of thing.'

'Cuddling is just for young people like you, is it?' I asked with a grin.

Margaret gave me a glare.

It seemed to us that she spent more of her time at dinners and parties than lectures, although she said that was nonsense. If she was still hopeful that a certain young doctor in Berkshire would realise she was the woman of his dreams, she certainly wasn't letting it stop her from having fun in the meantime.

'Talking of which,' I said. 'Among all the nice young men who send telegrams or flowers or letters to you every five minutes, is there a chemical genius?'

Margaret opened her mouth to retort, and then frowned.

'Why?'

'I'd like something analysed.'

She raised her eyebrows, and closed her mouth.

Into the silence shrieks of delight flowed from the bathroom. 'Papa pash! Eded pash! Enen pash!' I feared for the state of the floor, not to mention Gwen. If I was going to investigate properly, I had to know Ed would be well looked after. Tomorrow I would brace myself and hire a nanny. Preferably one less terrifying than Nanny Kincaid.

'I might do,' said Margaret. 'Isn't it something you ought to give to the police?'

'We shall,' I assured her. 'When we have proper evidence. At the moment it's too vague.'

Margaret frowned again. 'What is it you want analysed?'

I pulled out Father's bag of Crystal Kisses.

'Oh. Those.' My sister took one and rolled it in her hand. 'They're very popular with the male students.'

'What do *you* think of them?'

'Not my sort of thing,' she said. 'A bit too sweet for me. The boys swear by them — they say Crystal Kisses help them do their essays and burn the midnight oil and whatnot, but it seems too good to be true. Men are idiots. But yes, I know someone who'd do it. She's highly skilled.'

'She?'

'Women can be scientists too.'

'I know that.' I rolled my eyes. 'But you mostly talk about boys.'

'The boys don't take anything seriously,' said Margaret.

'At the moment they're constantly hungover. Dr Naylor's a lecturer, anyway. I can't ask her to do something like that. *You* can't ask her, either.'

'Why can't I?'

'She'd recognise you as my sister. Even if I wanted to get involved in one of your wretched investigations again — which I don't — I definitely don't want to get into trouble.'

'What about Connie?'

'She's your partner at the agency.'

'Reg?'

'Too young.'

'James?'

'Journalist.'

'All right, Albert?'

Margaret gave me a withering look. 'Honestly?'

I thought for a while. Perhaps we could hire an extra member of staff. That would free Connie and me up to do what we wanted to do — or rest.

Margaret selected one of the sweets and held it to the light. It was an odd swirly blue as if it were full of clouds.

'This is a strange one,' said Margaret. 'It looks like a crystal ball.' She threw it into the fire where it sparkled for a while and then started to melt.

Crystal ball…

'Ernestine Bugg!' I exclaimed, jumping up to go and telephone Connie.

'Who?' said Margaret.

'Another pair of hands,' I answered. 'And just the pair we need.'

CHAPTER 7
Connie

'I hope she still lives here,' I said, as Tredwell pulled up outside a neat little row of terraces in Wandsworth.

'It doesn't look any different,' said Katherine. 'Then again, it's been three or four years since we last came. Anything could have happened.'

We had debated the best way to get hold of Ernestine Bugg for some time. A letter explaining what we wanted might fall into the wrong hands. We had sought her alter ego, Bassalissa, among the posters and handbills which still advertised mediums and clairvoyants in the little theatres off Drury Lane, but she had vanished. The only option left was to call, and hope for the best.

'Here goes,' said Katherine, as we approached number eight. Was I imagining it, or had the curtains been changed?

A flustered young woman answered the door, her hair

tied in a scarf and a bonny toddler balanced on her hip. Her eyes flicked over us. 'Can I help you?' she asked, shifting the toddler slightly. 'Don't wriggle, Rosie.'

'I'm terribly sorry to bother you,' I said, 'but we were looking for a Mrs Bugg who used to live here.'

'She's moved on,' the woman said flatly. 'Been gone two years.'

'Oh.' Katherine and I looked at each other. 'I don't suppose you have an address for her?'

But the woman was peering at us with a little smile on her face. 'Well I never!' She chuckled to herself.

'Is something amusing you?' Katherine asked, drawing herself up to her full height.

'She's got you two to a T,' said the woman, and giggled. 'A little carroty woman and a big fancy-dressed one, she said, a real odd couple. An' with funny names, too.' She tickled the toddler, who gurgled happily. 'Go on, tell me your names.'

'Miss Caster and Miss Fleet,' said Katherine, with a resigned little sigh.

'Hee hee! Wait there a minute.' The woman manoeuvred herself and the toddler out of the doorway, and returned with a visiting card. 'She said if you was ever to come, I should give you this.'

I took the card — a thick, cream-coloured pasteboard with a spray of irises in the corner — and we read it together.

Mrs Ernestine Hamilton
2A, Craven Lane, Bayswater
At home Tuesday and Thursday afternoons

Now it was Katherine's turn to laugh. 'We've come all this way, and she lives half a mile from me!' We thanked our informant and I gave her a silver sixpence for Rosie, who waved it enthusiastically as we walked back to our carriage.

***

Given Ernestine's change in circumstances, we decided it best to send in our visiting cards before facing her in her den on Tuesday. That task done, we repaired to Katherine's to discuss the next move.

'Reg is getting background on Fraser's,' I said. 'I sent him to the library to do some reading up. Oh, and I've told him not to eat any more of the Crystal Kisses. Not that I needed to, but you never know.'

'Mm.' Katherine got up and rang for tea. 'What did Jemima say?'

'I didn't have long to talk to her alone. She had to go up to the nursery because baby Millie wouldn't settle, and Joseph refused to nap at all.'

'How old is he, four?' Katherine narrowed her eyes. 'Is this what I have to look forward to?'

'Ed barely naps now,' I retorted. 'You'll be a seasoned campaigner by the time he's four. I mentioned Crystal Kisses and she said that Joseph loves them. She thinks it's the colours, but apparently her nanny told her that he points to them in shop windows, and to the posters, and begs her for just one.'

'Oh no.'

'Don't worry, Jemima's strict about sweets. She let the nanny get him a ha'penny worth once, as a special treat, and after eating them he wouldn't go to bed. Apparently he didn't sleep at all that night. So no more Crystal Kisses for young Master Joseph.'

Tamar the maid arrived and Katherine requested tea and cake. 'Did you do the — other thing?' she asked, once the maid had departed.

I grinned. 'Yes, I did.'

'What did Albert say?'

'He was pleased to be asked. And yes, he's agreed.'

'Wonderful.' Katherine sank into the armchair and sighed contentedly. 'I feel as if things are coming together.'

That morning, after breakfast, I had entered the study with trepidation. 'Are you busy?' I asked Albert, who was sitting at a desk covered with piles of paper.

He looked up and smiled. 'Yes I am, and I would *love* a distraction, so I hope you have one for me.'

'Ooh good,' I said, sitting down. 'I hope so. It is sort of connected.'

'That'll have to do,' said Albert, putting the paper he was holding on one of the piles. 'Go on, Connie.'

'Weeelll… I was wondering if you could make some business enquiries into Fraser's.'

'The confectioners?' Albert frowned. 'It's hardly my usual line of investment.'

'I know,' I said, my heart sinking, 'but you might know someone, through your club, or your business associates —'

Albert's frown vanished as quickly as it had come. 'As I said, it really isn't in my line. And if people get talking, they'll trace my interest back to you and the agency like *that.*' He snapped his fingers. 'But I know a man I can ask.'

I put my elbows on the desk. 'Who?'

'Anstruther at the bank. He's discreet, and he has fingers in all sorts of pies. I can trust him to be confidential — not just about us, but he won't breach other people's trust either. It also fits rather well with something I had planned. In fact, I'm meeting with him this afternoon, so I'll add it to my list.'

'You're an angel,' I said, leaning across the desk and kissing him.

'Mind the paperwork!' he said, mock-severely. A few kisses later, most of it was on the floor...

'*Connie!*'

I came back to reality to find Katherine waving a piece of fruitcake in front of me. 'Ooh sorry, I was miles away,' I said, taking it from her. 'Lovely.'

'I'm sure it was,' she said, with a wink. 'Tamar asked if you were sickening for something.'

I sipped my tea, which Katherine had poured for me in readiness. 'Speaking of which, it's nice to see you looking so much brighter.'

'I *feel* brighter,' Katherine said. 'I don't know why it's taken me so long.'

'Babies are hard work,' I said, reflectively. 'I'm not sure how many more I can manage. Heaven knows how Mother did it.'

'Your mother is made of whalebone and steel,' said Katherine, choosing a slice of cake. 'There's nothing she can't handle.'

'Mm,' I said. 'I hope I'm the same.'

***

2a Craven Lane turned out to be the bottom two floors of a large white townhouse facing a little green. We were admitted by a neat parlourmaid, and shown to a drawing room with good furniture and no trace of the Arabian Nights flavour so conspicuous in Bassalissa's front room.

'I'm not sure how this will go,' whispered Katherine, as the parlourmaid disappeared to find her mistress.

But though she wore navy silk, and her hair was fashionably dressed, it was the same Ernestine Bugg who came into the room, her green eyes glinting and a broad grin on her face. 'I wondered how long it'd take you to find me,' she said. 'I've told Baxter to bring us tea.'

'What happened to Bassalissa, Ernestine?' I asked, glancing round the well-appointed room.

'Well,' said Ernestine, settling herself in an armchair. 'One day Bassalissa had a client, a middle-aged, well-to-do, sensible man who was at his wits' end. "I want to know if I'll ever meet a sensible woman I can love," he said. I told him he was probably looking in the wrong places, and from that point we got on like a house on fire.'

'I see,' said Katherine. 'And he made you stop being Bassalissa when you married?'

Ernestine grinned. 'That was my decision. It didn't seem the thing, not here. Oh, and I go by Tina now, not Ernestine.' She looked reflective. 'When I was struggling in Wandsworth I felt I needed a bigger name; but now I'm comfortable, it seems much more natural to be Tina. And Mr Hamilton likes it.' She smiled. 'Don't worry though, I still give advice.'

'How?' I tried to imagine a refined version of Bassalissa, and gave up.

Baxter arrived, bearing a tray laden with tea-things and bread and butter. 'I'll bring the cake-stand, ma'am.'

'Thank you, Baxter. Oh, and could you bring today's *Messenger*?' Baxter bobbed, and returned two minutes later with the cake stand and a somewhat crumpled newspaper.

'Here,' said Ernestine, turning to a page with its corner folded down.

'Oh, I love *Mrs Minchin Answers*!' I said. 'She's so polite to the people who write in with their dilemmas, and at the same time really quite rude. It's such a refreshing change from all the proper news about hostilities and skirmishes in places I've never even heard of. Do you read her, too?'

Ernestine couldn't have grinned any wider if she'd tried. 'I *am* her,' she said. 'You should see my postbag.'

'Of course you are,' said Katherine, faintly. 'Connie, could you hand me a sandwich or two?'

'With pleasure,' I said, taking a plate and adding one of every sandwich except the thinly-sliced beef. 'So, Ernestine, as you're so good at solving problems, could you help us with one?'

Ernestine snorted. 'Like I said, you should see my postbag. I answer letters on Monday and Wednesday, and write the column on Friday morning. If you want a problem solving, best write in.' She reached for the teapot with an air of finality.

So that was that. We would have to try elsewhere. I ate

my sandwiches quickly, keeping up a stream of chat on how lovely it was to see her again, none of which, I imagine, fooled Tina one bit. Katherine, meanwhile, worked through her plateful with difficulty, and I regretted giving her so much.

A bang on the front door made us look up. Then another, and another, then fists beating and a tearful voice. 'Ma, come quick!'

'Tilly!' Tina hurried to the door, and we followed.

Tilly, now a shade taller than her mother, grabbed Tina's hand. 'You have to help, Ma, you have to stop her!'

'Stop who?' asked Tina, as Tilly pulled her down the street.

'We were bowling our hoops on the green and Agnes's ran away so she chased it, and she got it just as it went into the road, but her sweets went into the gutter and she stopped to get them and oh, a horse an' carriage knocked her over!' Tilly paused for breath. 'But she's still in the road and we can't make her get up!' And she pointed to a little figure kneeling in the road, blood trickling down her face, oblivious to the carriages and bicycles and shouts, gathering something into her pinafore. Two more little girls stood by, weeping.

'Good heavens,' said Tina, and broke into a run. 'What are you doing, you silly child?' she cried, and yanked the child onto the pavement, spilling her sweets in the process.

'Get off me!' yelled Agnes, wriggling. 'I'd nearly got them all, and now I have to start again!'

Tina's eyes followed hers to the gutter, where brightly-coloured sweets glistened like jewels. 'These things!

They're a pestilence! I don't know why your mother lets you have them!' Her eyes narrowed. 'She doesn't, does she?'

Agnes, her chest heaving, stared at Tina, then broke free and dashed into the road, almost colliding with a bicycle.

'I know what to do,' said Tilly, stepping up. 'Agnes! Come here and we'll buy you two pennyworth of Crystal Kisses!'

That grabbed Agnes's attention. 'Promise?' she said, from the gutter.

Tilly looked at Tina, who nodded. 'Promise,' she said. 'Please come here.' And Agnes allowed herself to be led home, where she was received with horror by the nanny, who had been seeing to the baby and consequently had missed all the excitement. 'Don't forget my Crystal Kisses!' Agnes said to us, as the door closed.

We went back to Tina's house, and she dispatched Baxter to get the sweets. 'I'd send Tilly if it was anything else,' she said, 'but I don't want her trying those things.'

'She's too sensible,' I said. 'The apple doesn't fall far from the tree.'

Tina smiled, briefly. 'That's true.'

'Now about our problem,' said Katherine. 'If I said it was concerning Crystal Kisses, would you be interested?'

Tina's green eyes looked from one to the other of us. Then she lifted the teapot and filled our cups. 'I'm all ears,' she said.

Chapter 8
Katherine

I was playing hide and seek with Ed before work the following morning when a knock sounded at the door of my study.

'Are you in here, ma'am?' called Tamar's soft voice. I considered pretending I wasn't but Ed shouted 'Mamamama' and presumably pointed because the next thing I knew, Tamar's serious face peered round the desk and blinked at the sight of me squeezed into the hollow space underneath.

As usual, she showed little other expression, but I saw a slight redness around her eyes. I wondered what was wrong. We had a happy house. The maids got on well, Ada ran a steady ship, and they all actively discouraged me from helping with the housework. Whether that was because I got in their way, or my work wasn't up to their standard, I wasn't sure. The only task which anyone handed over with relief was Ed when he was having a particularly energetic day.

'You seem upset, Tamar,' I said, extracting myself as elegantly as I could. 'Is there a problem at home?' I lifted Ed into my lap, where — James's son to a T — he started pulling out my hairpins.

'Everyone's fine, ma'am.' Tamar's lip wobbled nonetheless.

'Is your young man —' I wondered how to finish the sentence. Tamar was the only person, apart from presumably his mother, who liked him. I had encountered him in the kitchen once or twice and noted his shifty glance, as if he were about to steal some cheese or nibble at the heel of the loaf.

'He's orl right, ma'am.' Tamar sniffed. 'Working a lot at present.'

I wasn't sure what to make of that, but before I could ask, she swallowed and came to the point. 'Ada says you're after another maid. I thought — I thought you'd have too many staff and let me go. As I'm the newest.' A tear ran down her cheek.

'Oh goodness, Tamar, of course I wouldn't! Susan can't manage all four floors on her own and Ada's too —' I wanted to say *too old*, but if Ada ever found out there would be trouble. 'Ada's too busy in the kitchen. It's just that Ed is hard work for Gwen on her own and I can't be here all the time. I have work to do.'

It seemed a feeble excuse to make to a girl whose mother managed eleven children and a laundry business with little help from anyone. But if Tamar thought the same, she made no indication. Her shoulders relaxed and she rubbed the tear away. 'Oh I'm glad ma'am. I'm saving.'

'That's good,' I said.

'I'm investing it so I can get married, ma'am.'

Before I could ask anything more Tamar had skipped from the room, and Gwen came in to collect Ed so that I could go to the office.

***

James came with me in a cab, holding my hand like he had in our early courtship but staring out of the window in silence, as he always did when something was on his mind.

It seemed he was still not quite ready to tell me what was wrong, so I told him about the conversation with Tamar.

He raised his eyebrows. '*Investing* is an odd word for Tamar to use. How much are we paying her?'

'Not enough for Albert's sort of investments,' I said. 'I imagine she means a savings bank or a building society. I just hope she's not handing it over to her young man. Ada's a good judge of character and she won't even let him past the back gate.'

'Good judge of character?' snorted James. 'She always thought I'd corrupt you with shenanigans and I'm a perfect gentleman.'

'If she really thought that, she'd have beaten you down the steps with a broom and locked me in my room.' I squeezed his hand and hazarded a guess. 'How are things at the paper?'

'Good,' said James. 'More than good. I've decided to

take a few days' leave and let the sub-editor show me what he can do.'

'Oh!' I felt disappointed. We'd already planned to go to the seaside once the case was finished, but here was James taking leave when he knew I'd be busy, and maybe later, when I was free, he wouldn't be. He turned to look at me properly, and he had a sheepish air about him. I waited for him to say he was going to finish his novel while Connie and I pored over Reg and Tina's research. I wouldn't have minded so much if he'd let me read the wretched thing.

He nudged me out of my reverie. 'Please Mrs King, I wondered if you'd give me a job.'

'What? I mean pardon?'

'Go on,' he urged. 'I'm a good worker, not afraid to get my hands dirty… You said you wanted to go back to the old days and I fancy helping out. Here's your chance. We can gallivant in cabs and maybe even have the odd cuddle at the same time.'

I giggled as his arm came round me. 'I can only pay you in kisses,' I said.

'Sounds good to me, but I'm very expensive,' he answered with a wink. 'I might need more than a kiss.' Then his face sobered a little. 'There is a reason I want to help. It's not just because of what you've found out so far, it's to do with something one of the paper's reporters has found out. Do you mind?'

'Not at all,' I said. 'The more the merrier.'

***

Our little office was full to bursting. Reg and James sat on the desks while Connie, Tina and I took the chairs. It was warm for once, and the fire seemed superfluous.

'You needn't call me Mrs Hamilton, either,' said Tina when James introduced himself. 'Call me by my first name . . . or Mrs Minchin!' She giggled. 'Don't suppose you know who she is, though.'

'I certainly do,' said James, grinning. 'I read her every week in case she gives me the solution to my problem.'

Connie held up her notebook. I hadn't had the chance to explain James's presence, but she didn't seem to mind. 'It's very nice to have your company Mr King, but please stop stealing all the sugar cubes. Now, let's bring the meeting to order,' she said. 'Tasks: Tina, you will approach St Kimbrose's Teaching Hospital and ask Dr Naylor for an analysis of the sweets. Reg, you will find out who prints the posters for Fraser's before perhaps going to the factory. Katherine and I shall go to the music hall?' She looked at me with a half-smile. I gave her a nod and then realised that the query in her voice might apply to herself.

'I've an appointment arranged with Dr Naylor at half past eleven,' said Tina. 'I am a worried mother and citizen who won't go to male scientists because they'll tell me I'm a fool.'

'I've got a few leads for printers.' Reg's expression changed from proud to worried. 'Not sure I'll manage the factory today as well and besides, they might get a bit suspicious.'

'I could go to the factory,' said James.

'As a reporter?' Connie frowned. 'It's too early for that. I don't mean to suggest you'd be unprofessional, James. It's just that if something *is* wrong, a reporter could make them cautious before we can find out, and then we've no hope.'

James shook his head. 'No. I'd go incognito and ask for an office job.' He looked at his hands. 'I've been idling about too much recently to be someone they'd take into the factory proper, and I can't cook.' Reg grinned but James didn't. 'I haven't properly had the chance to explain even to Katherine. I'd like to help Caster and Fleet on this case and there's a reason why. Mrs, erm, Tina, you may not know what I do, but —'

'You're the editor of *The Worker's Voice,*' said Tina. 'Very good paper, too.'

'Thank you. Well, yesterday evening one of my reporters gave me a piece he'd written. He's been investigating overcrowding — twenty families to one privy, that sort of thing — with a view to exposing the landlords. The level of sickness in those places is appalling. The children are too ill to go to school, and they're one step away from the workhouse with little hope of improving their lives. That's not new, regrettably, but we won't stop reporting it until things change. However, yesterday there *was* something new. The children and young people, sick and poor as they are, are fixated with Crystal Kisses. All the adults told him the same thing. Not just fixated, but getting them.'

'Who can begrudge them a bit of luxury?' asked Connie, but I knew she was thinking the same as me. *Fixated.*

'No-one,' said James.

Tina and Reg sighed simultaneously.

'I'm not judging,' said Tina. 'They might be nicking the

sweets. I mean, who'd blame them. All the same, that's the only way unless —' Her face darkened. 'Here — it's not just the pretty kids that are getting the sweets, is it?'

James shook his head. 'I know what you're thinking, but no. Neither thieving, nor lures, nor "rewards". And it's always Crystal Kisses. Those are the ones they want.'

'They're a bit like that,' said Reg. 'I only had a few and they were 'orrible, but it was two days before I didn't want more anyway.'

'Perhaps their parents are putting money aside for them,' said Connie. 'Sweets aren't expensive.' She pondered a bit harder. 'Although if these are the families your paper reports on, where no child has shoes and there are no blankets and one set of clothes each, saving even a penny is a sacrifice.'

'It's worse than that,' said James. 'They're so poor they scrounge stripped bones from the butcher on a Saturday night so they can boil them with potatoes for the flavour of meat on Sunday. They can barely afford the potatoes. My reporter asked as carefully as he could how they could afford sweets and the answer was, they didn't. Once a week, someone gives them away for nothing. The children just have to know where to go and what to say. No strings, no catch, nothing to do in exchange. As you say, Connie, who'd begrudge them the luxury?' He paused. 'But what those children need is food, not sweets. And they're being trained to crave them.'

CHAPTER 9
Connie

'Why would anyone give sweets away?' I asked, as the cab rattled towards Lambeth.

'To give people a taste for them,' said Katherine. 'Look how well it works at the Merrymakers.'

'I know that,' I said, frowning. 'But not just at the beginning. More and more, and only to children who know where to go and what to say... It's almost as if...'

Katherine turned to face me. 'As if what?'

'As if it was a sort of secret club. It doesn't make sense. Not if they want to get more people eating Crystal Kisses.'

'Mm. Although... Connie, you never went to school, did you?'

'No, we had a governess and masters. I read every school story I could find though. It sounded *wonderful*.'

'Wait until you've tried it,' said Katherine, darkly. 'In the stories you read, was there ever a secret club or society?'

'Yes!' I beamed. 'And they met at midnight, and had feasts, and the most popular girls were invited, and then someone who wasn't invited sneaked in and spoilt it and they got discovered —'

'That's exactly it,' said Katherine. 'If there's a rumour of a secret, *any* child would want to be in on it. Oh, how crafty they are…' She seemed to see for miles, and her face took on a set, stern expression until we pulled up outside the Merrymakers Music Hall. Merrymakers, indeed. That was the last emotion either of us were feeling.

***

'You two, *again*,' said Mr Templeton in disbelief. 'Wot 'ave I done to deserve this? On re'earsal day an' all.'

Ron had shown us straight into the auditorium, where we found Mr Templeton sitting at a table nursing a mug of tea while a troupe of acrobats moved listlessly through their routine.

'I'm sorry if we've come at a bad time,' I ventured.

'It's never a good time with you two,' he growled. 'When I see your faces I know I'm in for trouble. What is it this time?'

'We want to know the name of the traveller who visited you about the Crystal Kisses,' said Katherine. 'Oh, and if you have anything on paper, we'd like to see it.'

'Would you now,' said Mr Templeton, his eyes on the stage. 'Look lively, you lot!' he barked. 'This is a music hall not the Queen's funeral, Gawd bless 'er.' Then he sighed. 'Awright. If it gets you out of me hair, what's left of it. *Ron!*'

Ron, who had been leaning on the door-frame, watching proceedings, strolled over. 'Wot?'

'Wot *sir*. There's a pink envelope in the top drawer of my desk. Bring it to me, would yer.'

'Sir yes *sir*.' Ron saluted, clicked his heels, and marched off.

'That boy.' Mr Templeton shook his head. 'All right you lot, get off. I've seen enough. Too much, in fact. Get yourselves sharpened up for tonight. An' tell Selina she's on next.'

The youngest acrobat, a scrawny girl, paused in her shuffling. 'Selina ain't in yet,' she piped.

'Wot? She knows what day it is!'

The girl's left foot made little circles on the floor. 'Well, she ain't.'

'Fine. Betty an' Buster, then.' The girl nodded assent and made herself scarce. Betty and Buster appeared, bright and brisk, and began their routine.

Presently Ron sidled into the auditorium. ''Ere you are,' he said, and handed a long sugar-pink envelope to Mr Templeton.

'Thankee.' Mr Templeton withdrew a single piece of sugar-pink paper from the envelope and glanced over it. 'Nothin' there I'm ashamed to share wiv yer,' he said, and dropped it on the table.

Katherine and I skimmed the sheet. It was all there, just as Mr Templeton had said: the agreement to supply the song, a payment for every night Ellen sang it, an allowance of five pounds of Crystal Kisses per night for distribution among the audience and performers, and a discount of fifty per cent on the trade price of the sweets, for retail at the music hall. Delivery of the sweets to take place weekly before one o'clock on Saturday, ready for the matinee.

Katherine read aloud. '*This agreement remains in force until one or other party expresses a wish to break it. No penalty will be suffered for doing so, on either side.*' She looked at Mr Templeton. 'I don't suppose there's anything we can say —'

'No,' replied Mr Templeton. 'Awright Betty, you're on form. And you, Buster. Tell the dancers they're on.'

Betty curtsied, Buster barked, and she tripped off with Buster trotting at her heels.

I read through the document again. 'Surely not.' At the bottom, underneath Mr Templeton's sprawling, looped signature, was a neat little inscription. '*A. Sweet Esq, for Fraser's*'.

'Yeah, we 'ad a laugh about that, me and 'im,' remarked Mr Templeton. ''E said it must have been Fate that drew 'im into confectionery. Not that he eats much of it, I'll bet. Scrawny little man. Pleasant, though. And neat, very neat.'

'What did he look like?' I asked.

Mr Templeton's eyes narrowed. 'I'm not setting you two on the poor man. He's just doing his job. If you're that interested, why don't you enquire at Fraser's factory?'

The dancers were trooping on stage, adjusting their costumes, and getting into position. I craned my neck to look for Selina, but I couldn't see her. I was about to nudge Katherine when Selina ran on, adjusting her shoulder strap. She looked dreadful — pale, thin, and haunted. Her hair was up all anyhow, and a hole gaped in the calf of her tights.

'What time d'yer call this, Selina?' bellowed Mr Templeton.

Selina turned huge, hollow eyes on him. 'I overslept.'

'Pull the other one. You don't look like you've been to bed at all.'

Selina stood, fidgeting.

'Go on!' Mr Templeton shouted.

'Play our first number,' Selina muttered to the band, and they scraped and blew into life.

As the introduction began the dancers' necks lengthened, they stood taller, their arms curved into grace, and, after a few seconds, they moved as one.

All except Selina, who stumbled through her movements like a sleepwalker until she tottered and fell, nearly crushing Linnie.

The rest of the dancers cast a guilty eye at Mr Templeton then clustered round Selina, loosening the collar of her costume, stroking her hair, patting at her face. 'I think she's fainted,' one of them called.

Katherine and I hurried towards the stage. I did not dare to look at Mr Templeton.

Selina was out cold, and as motionless as a statue. 'Somebody get her a glass of water. Brandy, if it's available,' called Katherine. 'And a blanket or a wrap.' She felt for a pulse. 'Her heart is beating very fast.'

Presently a shudder, then another, ran through Selina's whole frame. 'Not time to get up,' she murmured, and curled into a ball.

We heard the scrape of a chair, and Mr Templeton loomed over us. 'How dare you turn up to work in such a state!' he yelled. 'Is this what I pay you for?'

Katherine glared at him. 'Now is not the time,' she snapped.

'It bloody well is!' he spluttered. 'You haven't had to put up with her coming in late, twitching like a startled rabbit all the time she's on stage, and then stopping in the bar till we have to throw her out to close up. I've had enough!'

Selina's shoulders began to heave.

'I've a good mind ter —' He stopped at the tap of heels on the boards behind him. Ellen stood there, in the cerise dress we had seen her wear a few days ago, and holding a coat.

She walked closer, and looked down at Selina. Then she held out a hand. 'Come on. I'm taking you home.'

Selina shuddered again. 'Got to dance. Can't go home.'

Ellen sighed. 'You're no use to anyone in this state, you silly cow. You helped look after me once, when I was in trouble, and now I'm going to look after you.' She crouched, got hold of Selina's hand, and pulled her into a sitting position, then draped the coat around her shoulders. 'There's brandy under the bar,' she said to one of the dancers. 'Or the second drawer of Mr T's filing cabinet.' Two dancers rushed in different directions, glad to have something to do.

'Ere!' exclaimed Mr Templeton. 'That's for personal use!'

'Well if you 'adn't brought those damn Crystal Kisses

in then she wouldn't need it, would she?' Ellen said, her West Country accent rich as cream. 'I bet she hasn't eaten a thing since she left here yesterday, except for a few handfuls of sweets. Have you?'

Selina shook her head. 'Wasn't hungry,' she murmured.

'See?' Linnie returned with a large tumbler of brandy, and Ellen helped Selina drink a little. 'Not too much,' she warned. 'Don't want you drunk as well as incapable.'

Selina managed a watery smile.

Ellen stood, and, small as she was, squared up to Mr Templeton, who seemed to have shrunk by comparison. 'I ain't singing that song no more, Mr T. I refuse. You can get someone else to do it, but if you've any sense, you won't.'

'We'll see about that,' muttered Mr Templeton, but he looked uneasy, as if the boards beneath him might give way at any time.

'An' if you're smart you'll rip up whatever agreement you've put your name to, and tell these two ladies everything you know.' Ellen nodded in our direction. 'Otherwise I have a feelin' you could end up with a bigger problem than one fainting lady.'

'Are you threatening me?' said Mr Templeton, quietly, and it was worse than if he had screamed in her face.

But Ellen stood her ground. 'No, Mr Templeton. I'm tellin' you, and you oughta listen.' She stared at him with her big blue eyes until he looked away. 'Someone get a cab. I'm goin' to take her home an' put her to bed. I'll see you this evening.'

Selina was gathered up, put onto her feet, and between two dancers, walked to a waiting cab. 'Sorry,' she whispered as they manhandled her in.

'We must talk to her,' I murmured to Katherine, as Ellen got into the cab. 'When she's a bit better.'

Ellen stuck her head out of the window. 'Mr T!'

Mr Templeton stood on the steps, arms folded. He raised his head at Ellen's salutation. 'What now?'

'You've got some working out to do. She ain't coming back tonight, so you're an act down. Better get your thinking cap on!' With a final cheery wave she disappeared from view, and the cab drove away.

CHAPTER 10
Katherine

The remaining cast shuffled its feet.

Mr Templeton glared at everyone in turn. 'Where's Gert? She sorta knows Selina's act. Nan, you can stand in for Ellen: get on with it.'

A short, curvaceous dancer gasped out 'I've lost me voice Mr T, and Gert's at her gran's funeral.'

'Then she needn't bother coming back. That's the fifth gran that's died since Christmas.' Mr Templeton almost bit the end off his cigar in irritation. 'What about the rest o' yer? Where's your ambition?'

Linnie looked up. 'Maybe I —'

'I know, I know,' said Betty, bouncing a little in excitement. 'Felicity Velour could sing the Crystal Kisses song. I mean Miss F could sing and Miss C could mime, like they did before. You'd do that, wouldn't yer?'

'Yeah?' said Mr Templeton. 'Both of you are sprogged

up now, ain't yer? Yer 'usbands'd let you prance about on stage? And what about Selina's spot?'

There was no question that the sparkle had gone from most of the troupe. I swallowed and exchanged glances with Connie, who gave a minuscule nod.

'We'll step over here and discuss it while you — encourage them,' I said, and led Connie towards the wings as Mr Templeton continued his harangue.

'You want us to go back on stage, don't you?' she said. 'Just because you feel bad about the cast.'

'I'm not sure,' I said. A tiny part of me sparkled, dreaming of being on stage again — not a mother, nor a wife, but silly, outrageous Felicity Velour. The other part of me felt exhausted even imagining it and wanted to curl up under a blanket.

Connie bit her lip. 'We could,' she whispered. 'I think we could.' She wore the same encouraging look as she had on the day Mr Maynard came round, and she gave me the tiniest wink.

'It's not just that,' I answered. 'We might be able to further the case.'

'How?'

'We can sing the Crystal Kisses song.'

Connie frowned. 'But then we're encouraging sales.'

'Not if we change the words to send a different message.'

Connie's face cleared a little. 'Oh I see. That doesn't help with Selina's act, though. We can't do that.'

'We can ask Tina if she'd resurrect Bassalissa.'

Connie shook her head. 'She's put all that behind her.'

'I know, but I'm sure she'd be game. We can but ask and if she says no, she says no. The same goes for you. If you say no, we won't.'

'Oh, I'm game,' said Connie. 'Selina is our friend. I don't know if it'll make a difference. But it's worth a try.'

We stepped forward a little. 'M-Mr Templeton…'

He glared at us. 'What is it? I'm turning into a camel cos you two give me the 'ump. You only show up when there's trouble and — 'ang on —' his eyes narrowed. 'If you're not careful I'll actually *get* a camel costume and put you both in it. That'd raise a smile, but it's not jokers I'm short of. I hope.' Dan Datchett cringed under Mr Templeton's scowl. 'I need a good singer and a pretend medium ready to tread the boards in six hours — so what you gonna do about that?'

'If Ron will send some telegrams for us,' I replied, 'we might have the answer.'

***

James and Reg met us in a Lambeth pie shop at five. James was still in the black second-hand ready-made suit he wore when undercover as a clerk. A huge brown teapot and five mugs were placed in the middle of the table along with four dishes full of pie and mash. Connie, who had declined the food, turned almost as green as the parsley-speckled gravy and moved her chair slightly so that she couldn't see me eat. I, however, was ravenous and even the possibility of eels couldn't put me off the buttery potato. Four years had passed since I'd last danced on a stage and I'd forgotten how exhausting it was. Tina, cradling her mug, watched me with a small grin and I surreptitiously wiped my chin in case there was gravy on it.

'I don't know where to start,' said James. 'Reg and I thought we'd come back at four to an office full of chattering women, and all we find is a couple of telegrams saying the three of you are at the Merrymakers. What are you all doing? And what does Albert say about it?'

Connie winced a little. 'He said he'd join you to watch and we'd better be good. I'm taking that as approval. It seemed wisest.'

I gave a brief summary of what had happened when we arrived at the theatre.

'And *I* got back to the office at two,' said Tina, applying her cutlery to the food, 'to find a telegram saying *Bring Bassalissa to the Merrymakers*. Who could resist that? Only I'll be Madame Mystericon. Bassalissa never made anything up.' She popped a mouthful of mutton pie in her mouth and winked.

'I'm still confused,' said James.

'Tina's adapting her old persona for the stage,' I said. 'You wait. Connie and I are copying Ellen and adjusting her song to see what reaction we get. Hopefully it'll have been worth missing bedtimes and earning the wrath of our nursery staff.'

'Oh, don't,' said Connie, her mouth turned down. 'I've told Albert it's just one night. It *has* to be worth it. After this Ellen's understudy can do the song even if I have to pour medicine down her throat myself.'

I knew how she felt. I too felt sad I'd miss my baby's sleepy little eyelids drooping as he fell into slumber.

'So anyway,' I said. 'How did you two get on? Tina's

successfully handed over the sweets for analysis.'

'Dr Naylor was very interested,' confirmed Tina. 'Said we'd get the results by tomorrow.'

'Good for you,' said Reg, 'I still haven't found the printer. All the leads led up blind alleys. Literally. Gotta admit though —' He looked a little sheepish. 'I didn't actually go up some of the alleys. I ain't doing Whitechapel alone.'

Connie gasped. 'Goodness, no! You mustn't.'

'But I reckon it was a false trail anyway,' Reg continued. 'The posters all have a printer's name and address on the bottom — there are three as far as I can tell, but all the addresses are fake. Cavalle Street instead of Cavell Street, that sort of thing.'

'What happened to you, James?' said Connie.

'The manager at Fraser's seemed nice when he gave me an interview. He asked me what I knew about confectionery, and it's lucky I know nothing because he'd have spotted it if I had. I've been offered a job. Ten hours a day, six days a week for two pounds and ten shillings. I'd earn thirty shillings a week less in the factory. That's not bad.'

Connie looked at her watch and let out a small groan. 'Come on ladies, we've work to do.'

'Oh dear,' I sighed. 'The dress I have to wear is greener than this gravy.'

'Never mind the dress,' said James. 'Just get all the muck off your face before you leave the theatre. I'm going home to change into my second-best evening attire and I don't want paint on it.'

Connie took one last disgusted glance at my half-empty plate.

'You must be starving,' I said. 'They're sure to have food backstage.'

'I hope so,' Connie replied, but she looked as if it would take a while for her appetite to return.

***

Tina in the role of Madame Mystericon brought the house down. Starting with Connie, who wanted to know if she'd ever find true love, and working her way through a number of cast members who had conveniently found themselves sitting in the audience, she told 'fortunes' with the aid of a huge orb, expertly spotlighted so that it glowed with different colours depending on what she said. Each person brought a different query and received an increasingly ludicrous answer.

'Yer dead Uncle Cyril says look in the privy,' she told her final 'customer' — one of the male dancers — when he asked where his promised inheritance was.

'Ooh,' said the young man. 'In the privy? How strange. What should I look for?'

Madame Mystericon peered into the orb. 'I seeee — I seeeee — Yer Uncle Cyril says... Tell that boy to look deeep into the bowl and he will find . . . a big pile of exactly what he deserves!' The orb turned a deep brown and the curtain fell.

'Cor,' said Mr Templeton as Tina walked offstage with nonchalance. 'Wanna job?'

'I'll ask the spirits,' said Tina without expression. 'But once I've got this lot off, I'm going home. There's a child who'll want tucking in, if I know my Tilly.' And off she tripped, as if playing a fortune-teller in the music hall was part of a normal day.

'And we're on,' whispered Connie as the curtain rose again to display the city scene complete with advertisements for Crystal Kisses.

'Are you ready?' I asked.

Connie looked resolute. 'Yes.'

Dan Datchett bounded onstage. 'What's that I hear? Felicity Velour's back? What han honour! What's she got on her mind, I wonder?'

I danced onto the stage and did as good a pirouette as I could manage given the pie and mash which still lay heavily in my stomach. I pretended to give Dan a kiss on the cheek and then posed while the orchestra struck up the introduction to Ellen's song. My dress had such huge leg-o-mutton sleeves I feared I was wider than I was tall. Betty and the girls had had to stuff the bosom with stockings, as I was the only mother in history whose bust had got smaller since having a baby. I put a huge grin on my painted face and with a sideways glance at Connie, we launched into our version of the song.

My boy is sweeter than honey
That's supped from sugar cane,
And my heart becomes soft as marshmallow
Whenever he whispers my name.
I melt at his touch like chocolate,
I cannot resist his charms,
His kisses sparkle like sherbet

Whenever I'm in his arms.

No acid drops, no lemon pops,
No sour cherries indeed.
My boy gives Crystal Kisses
Instead of what I need.
I have a boy whose heart is true,
For a chocolate cream is just a dream
But who could wish for a Crystal Kiss?
Only a fool, that's who.

I waltzed for a couple of turns with the suave man in tails before the next verse.

Should I ignore his loving
When his gifts are too sweet and bright?
My heart beats so fast to the music
Throughout each shivery night.
His kisses and caresses enchant me —
I am lost and confused, you see.
I feel like a queasy princess
Whenever he's been with me.

No acid drops, no lemon pops,
No sour cherries indeed.
My boy gives Crystal Kisses
Instead of what I need.
I have a boy whose love's in doubt,
For a chocolate cream is just a dream
But who would wish for a Crystal Kiss?

Only a fool, that's who.

As I whirled in the arms of my 'lover' I looked up to the box where I knew James, Albert and Reg would be watching, and saw James waving at me and pointing. Before I could work out what he was trying to say I heard a frantic voice bellow:

'Fire! Fire! Get out! The theatre's on fire!'

CHAPTER 11
Connie

'You know when you said this would be a bit of fun...?' I asked Katherine, as we stood on the pavement outside the Merrymakers.

'Oh, do be quiet,' Katherine muttered, frowning with both her drawn-on eyebrows and her real ones. 'At least you've got proper clothes on.' She seemed to be trying to hide inside her coat.

The moment the word 'Fire!' was heard, there had been a stampede for the doors. The band had come to a hasty halt as their chairs were jostled and their instruments knocked in the rush.

'Everyone stay calm!' roared Mr Templeton, but it had no effect. Ron hurried to open both doors before they were battered down by the crush of people, and within a few minutes the auditorium was empty. Mr Templeton flicked us a glance. 'Out,' he said. 'I'm gonna check everyone's accounted for. I don't smell no —'

'There it is!' Ron pointed to a smoking ball of brown paper directly below the stage, where the band sat. He went over and stamped on it. 'Ugh,' he said, as his boot came away with half the bag stuck to it. 'It's those flaming Crystal Kisses. Gawd knows how that happened.'

Katherine and I looked at each other, and underneath the painted smile her mouth was set very firm indeed.

***

'I'm not saying it *was* your fault,' Mr Templeton clarified, as a cab drew up and Albert peered out. 'But you two attract trouble.' He sighed. 'There goes tonight's interval sales. I s'pose at least they all rushed off without asking for their money back. Everyone's safe, and the hall ain't burnt down. Let's call it a night.'

'Don't say a word,' Katherine said to James, as he handed her in, grinning.

'Who, me?' He sat beside her and put an arm round her shoulders. 'I think your dress is lovely.'

'At least we were allowed to go back in and get our belongings,' I said. 'Imagine if you'd had to go home with no hat and coat.'

'I'll go in first and warn Gwen,' James managed to choke out. 'I don't want Ed seeing you and having nightmares.'

I shot him a warning look but Katherine had already squirmed into the corner of the cab, and sat glowering, arms folded.

'If it helps, I thought your song was very good,' said Albert.

'Thank you, dear.' I smiled at him. 'Do you think it did any good, though?'

'It's hard to say. There was a bit of a stir when you sang the first chorus, sort of "Did she really say that?"'

'I suppose that's something,' said Katherine. 'Although I doubt we'll get to sing it again.'

I stared at her. 'You mean you want to? After tonight?'

One corner of Katherine's mouth curved up. 'It was still fun. I'm tired, though.' She sighed, and leaned her head against the window of the cab. I speculated on what the cabman would say when he found the smears of paint.

We dropped James and Katherine, well wrapped-up, at Joyce Square, and asked the cabbie to go on to Marylebone.

'I wonder who did it,' I said.

Albert gave me a gentle squeeze. 'You don't think it was an accident, then?'

I shook my head. 'Too much of a coincidence. And how can you set light to a bag of sweets by accident?'

'True. Hmmm...' I could hear the frown in Albert's voice. 'Someone near the front got up and walked out while Katherine was dancing. He was sitting near the band. I just assumed he didn't like the song, or he was offended — though why you'd sit through Dan Datchett and choose to walk out then...'

'What did he look like?' I asked eagerly.

'I couldn't see much, we were too high up. He was slight, and well turned out. A dapper little man.'

'*Mr Sweet*,' I breathed. 'How did he know we would change the words?'

Albert shrugged. 'Someone must have told him.'

'A spy.' A cold hand squeezed my heart. 'There's a spy at the Merrymakers.'

***

Once home I changed my dress which smelt of the music hall, and visited the nursery where, wonder of wonders, all the children were slumbering. I had hoped to nurse Lydia but she was emphatically asleep, her hands curled into tiny fists as if to fight anyone planning to disturb her. 'Have they been good?' I asked Lily.

'As gold, ma'am. Did you have a nice time at the music hall?'

'It was — interesting,' I said. 'Lily, might I ask you something?'

Her already pink cheeks flushed a little more. 'Of course, ma'am.'

'Do you know of any — investments — which are popular with servants?'

Lily looked rather relieved, and shook her head. 'I don't concern myself with anything like that, ma'am. I send a quarter of my wage home to Ma — I'd send more but she won't let me — I spend a quarter on clothes and boots and birthday presents, and the rest goes in the savings bank for a rainy day, or…' She bent her head, and her cheeks were very pink.

'I'm sorry, Lily, I didn't mean to embarrass you,' I said. 'I am very pleased with your work, but if, at some point, you decide to marry —'

'Thank you, ma'am,' she muttered, her head still bent.

'I'll, um, let you get on,' I said, and fled.

Albert was in the parlour, his tie loosened, reading the newspaper. 'Nancy's making cocoa,' he said. 'Do you want a cup?'

I shuddered. 'Heavens, no.' The thought of anything sweet turned my stomach. 'A cup of tea, perhaps. I'll ask when she comes back.' I sat beside him on the sofa and curled my feet under me. 'Anything interesting?'

'Double-checking the stocks.' Albert lowered the newspaper. 'Can you manage any more news, Connie?'

'It depends.' What was coming now? 'I can try.'

He laughed. 'It isn't anything as dramatic as tonight's happenings! It's just that I met with Anstruther again today. You remember I was going to ask him about Fraser's?'

'Oh yes.'

'It was a little surprising. They have a reputation as a family firm — very stable, Quaker, look after their workers, model housing and all that sort of thing. I thought they were wholly owned by the family.'

'Go on.'

'They were. Until about six months ago.'

I sat up, and Albert chuckled. 'An investor outside the family now has a fifty-one percent stake in the business. So that investor is the majority shareholder, and presumably decides what goes on.' He paused. 'Apparently the business had been failing, and this investor saved it — but at the cost of ultimate control for the family.'

'Do you know who it is?' I gasped. I had literally forgotten to breathe.

'There's the thing,' said Albert, mock-casually, laying

the newspaper on his lap. '*No-one* knows who it is. It's all done through a holding company. Not even the current Fraser himself knows. As you can imagine, Fraser's keep that quiet.'

'I'm sure they do.' My head was spinning. Shadowy investors, mysterious fire-starters — whatever next?

'You look absolutely exhausted, Connie.' Albert leaned over and kissed me. 'Why don't you have an early night? I'll be up soon. This detecting is hard work.'

***

I had expected not to sleep a wink, but I woke in the morning to birdsong and streaming light. 'Good morning, sleepyhead,' said Albert. 'There's tea in the pot.'

I struggled upright and peered at the clock. 'Half past eight! And I'm meant to be meeting Katherine in the office at ten!'

'You can always telephone —'

'*No.*' I threw back the covers and padded towards the tea tray.

In the end I was only ten minutes late. Katherine was already there, exceptionally well-scrubbed in an outfit with not a hint of green. 'You slept well, then,' she remarked, and I noticed the dark shadows under her eyes. 'James woke me up when he left for the factory.'

'Oh yes!' I told her Albert's news. 'Hopefully he'll spot something interesting.'

'Mm. I hope he passes. I'm not sure his writing could be described as copperplate. Although he did look quite clerk-like this morning.' Her tone suggested it wasn't a change she approved of.

'He'll be fine.' I hoped I sounded convincing; but last night had shaken me. 'Where's Reg?'

'Chasing up printers. He might have a friend or two with him as security.' Katherine pulled out the Crystal Kisses case file. 'I suppose we ought to write a report for Mr Maynard and tell him where we're up to.'

'Yes, we should.' I uncapped my fountain pen and began to jot down some headings. 'Do you know, I'd almost forgotten he'd asked us to get involved in the first place.'

'Me too,' said Katherine, coming to read over my shoulder. 'It seems — personal now.'

We spent the next three-quarters of an hour compiling a summary of our findings so far. 'I'll leave it for Reg to type,' I said, walking to his desk and placing it next to the typewriter. 'I know my limitations.'

A creak from below. Someone was coming upstairs. 'Maybe that's him,' I said.

But when the door opened, Tina's neat figure whisked inside. 'Morning,' she said.

'Good morning, Tina,' I replied. 'You missed some fun last night.'

'Mm,' she said, without interest. 'I've just come from Dr Naylor, at the hospital.'

'Oh!' Katherine cried. 'Has she given you the results?'

'She has.' Tina sat down and opened her bag. 'And you won't like it.' She drew out a long white envelope and extracted a typewritten sheet of paper. '*Crystal Kisses Analysis,*' she read. '*Ingredients, in order: Sugar, caffeine, citric acid, colourings (various including cochineal, all permitted), flavourings (vanillin, artificial fruit flavourings, all permitted), sodium (trace).'*

She paused.

'Warning: excessive consumption of Crystal Kisses may produce high levels of caffeine. This may cause irritability, disorientation, and inability to concentrate, especially combined with sugar. However, these sweets should not be considered dangerous, and there is no reason to remove them from sale.'

I sat down, abruptly.

'Dr Naylor didn't quite send me away with a flea in me ear,' Tina said, reflectively. 'And she didn't exactly say I'd wasted her time. But her expression did.'

'I can't believe there's nothing dangerous in those sweets,' I said, and my voice seemed to come from somewhere else. 'I know what I've seen.'

'So do I,' said Katherine. 'But a laboratory analysis says otherwise.' The shadows under her eyes seemed even darker. 'What do we do now?'

Chapter 12
Katherine

'What do we do now?' said Connie. 'We think. No more rushing head-first into things. No, actually, we go away and we *don't* think. And *then* we think.'

The trouble was that I had too many things on my mind to make sense of any of them. A pile of letters from prospective nursery staff waited at home. At breakfast, Tamar had looked dreadful and I wondered what to say if her young man had left her. James, wearing his lowliest junior clerk's suit, had gone to his new job very early. Ed had still been too sleepy to mind my leaving, which filled me with a mixture of relief and loss. To top it all, our report to Mr Maynard now had nothing important to say.

'Wait a moment,' said Tina, pausing as she placed the analysis on Reg's filing tray. 'I wasn't listening properly earlier. What did I miss last night? Did the change of words in the chorus cause trouble?'

Between us Connie and I explained about the fire that wasn't a fire.

'So if anyone noticed what we sang, they'll have forgotten,' I said, plucking at my gloves.

'It was a waste of effort,' Connie agreed.

'Don't you believe it,' said Tina. 'They might have shot themselves in the foot. Someone will say: "Weren't you at the Merrymakers when that fire happened? Tell me all about it," and the other person will start the story nice and slow to make it more dramatic than it was. As they're telling it, the change of chorus will come back to them. Ha!' She grinned. 'They haven't downed us yet.'

'You still think there's something in it?' I asked. 'Even with the analysis telling us the opposite of what we expected?'

'Oh yes.' Tina nodded. 'But Mrs Lamont is right. We need to go away and think.'

'We?' said Connie. 'You're still in it with us?'

'Oh dear me, yes.' Tina checked her reflection in the mirror over the hearth before turning to wink. 'Try leaving me out of it. But I do suggest a change. It'll be hard for me to do an act all the time. Tilly's at the sort of age it's hard to leave her, Mr Hamilton doesn't want me out every night and besides, I've got my Mrs Minchin work.'

Tina paused for breath, and Connie and I exchanged glances. 'The thing is, now I'm a lady of substance I support a lot of women's charities in London. I give talks and whatnot and —' She gave an enormous wink, 'I get lots of ideas for Mrs Minchin's column. Thing is, all sorts of women go to those meetings and gossip about everything from the vote to modern children to whether a hat can ever be too fancy. I could ask a ton of questions about Crystal Kisses and no-one would think it odd. It'll take me a while to get round them all, but let's see what the girls have got to say.' With a grin reminiscent of Reg, she bounced out of the door.

***

Connie was indeed right. It was a relief to have lunch with her like we used to, talk about domestic issues, then go home separately for two hours, in the hope that thinking about something else entirely would help dislodge whatever we were missing about the Crystal Kisses.

Gwen had taken Ed out by the time I arrived. I imagined her sitting with other nursery staff chatting without a care in the world while their charges, hopefully, napped in perambulators. I sometimes felt I'd picked the wrong career.

I settled in the study and stared in dismay at eight letters with my name scrawled in varying standards of literacy. My mind strayed to James, probably scribing away on a pitted desk. I wondered if it were a modern office with chairs or an old fashioned one with stools, and hoped any noise from the factory wouldn't drown out the noise of anyone creeping up on him with bad intent. *Stop thinking about the case*, I told myself. *James can look after himself.*

'Am I getting fat?'

Margaret's voice in the hall made me jump. I'd forgotten the medical school's spring term had ended.

'Stop being ridiculous,' said her friend Phoebe's voice. 'You're like a willow with a bosom. You only need boning for the latter, and you should know better than to lace your waist so tight.'

'Just because you prefer to go about almost *au naturel* doesn't mean I have to. Dr Naylor went on and on about corsetry yesterday too. At least she's got an excuse; she's old. Everyone over thirty is a little peculiar.'

'I thought you admired her.'

'I do,' said Margaret. 'But she was in a temper. I've no idea why, but it was a bore.'

'Speaking of peculiar,' said Phoebe, 'on the way here, I thought I saw your brother-in-law catching the tube, only it can't have been him. He looked rather down-at-heel and cut me completely.'

'He'll be out reporting on something grim. I daresay he thinks it makes it more real if he's in character. He's over thirty too. Come along, let's go.'

'Whatever do your neighbours think of Mr King leaving the house in costume?' asked Phoebe.

'We haven't cared what the neighbours think since 1890,' answered Margaret, her voice fading as they left the house. The door slammed.

I returned to my letters and read three applications, none filling me with confidence. I picked up the fourth. It didn't bode well that the envelope was grubby and a surname as simple as mine had been misspelled.

Dear Mrs Kinge, I wood like to apply for the post of nannie. I do not beleave in sparing the rod and —

I folded the letter back into its envelope and sighed.

'Here's something to keep you going till tea-time, Mrs Kitty.' Ada stood at the door with a small tray. On it was a teapot and cheese scones.

'Oh, Ada,' I said, putting my head in my hands. 'I know how to hire a housemaid but not a nanny. *I* didn't have a nanny. Mother and you brought me up. What am I supposed to look for?' Taking my hands from my face, I stared into hers. Ada had been there all my life. Two other maids had worked in the house until Father disappeared and I had to dismiss them, but Ada was as constant as the weather. I couldn't imagine life without her.

'Right,' said Ada. 'Hand those wretched letters to me.'

With a sigh of relief I passed them over so she could tell me whom to interview, but to my horror she threw the whole pile in the fireplace. The barely glowing coals flared up as the envelopes hit them, shooting two letters onto the hearth where their corners smouldered for a little and then went out. The remainder burned merrily, emitting inky smoke.

'Master Ed does *not* need a nanny,' said Ada. 'He's got you, he's got Gwen and he's got me. He'll start getting easier soon and he's a good lad. He's just full of beans as he ought to be. Would you prefer it if he sat like a doll?'

'But Ada,' I argued. 'You can't mind him and be cook-housekeeper. You should be retiring. And what if there's another —'

Ada's face turned beetroot-red. 'I'll retire over my own dead body,' she snapped without irony. 'This is not a big house like Mrs Lamont's. We can manage. And if you need to work out of the home I'll help look after Master Ed like he was my own, same as I did with you and Miss Meg. If he has to be in the kitchen peeling potatoes then where's the harm? It'll do him good not to be waited on hand, foot and finger. Now I'll take these scones to the drawing room where you'll eat them or there'll be trouble.'

She picked up the tray and stormed out.

Wondering for a second if she could solve the Crystal Kisses quandary too, I glanced at the clock. Connie would shortly be arriving so that we could go together to meet Reg at the office. The acrid smell of burning paper assaulted my nose. I rose to pick the last two letters from the hearth and put them on the fire. One was, unlike the others, typed. Curious, I ripped it open. Perhaps this applicant was more up to date.

Dear Mrs King

May I put myself forward as someone who would make an excellent nanny for your sweet little boy. I have been trained in all modern methods and believe in rewards not punishment. With a child as young as thirteen months, I can nurture the elemental —

Rolling my eyes, I threw the letter on the fire and went upstairs to the drawing room. Ada was right, we could manage without anyone else.

As I poured my tea Gwen and Ed came in, followed by Ada who was ushering in Connie. All of them looked fraught. Ed's little face was scarlet and his eyes wet, but he was silent as Gwen placed him in my arms and he snuggled his hot little head into my shoulder.

'Master Ed's got a slight fever, ma'am,' she said. 'I'm just telephoning for the doctor.'

'If it's all right with you, Mrs Kitty,' said Ada, 'could he see Tamar while he's here? I've had to send her to bed.'

'Oh no!' I exclaimed. 'Is it contagious? Connie, you must go home! What if I've already passed it on? And I can't go out, I —'

'Don't fret,' Connie reassured me. 'Maybe Ed is about to start teething again. What's wrong with Tamar?'

Ada's lips narrowed. '*She's* not got a fever. She's been sick until she's wrung out like a dish-rag. Her young man sent her a box of sweets and the greedy thing ate the lot. I'm hoping that's all it is and not that he's given her something else.'

Connie went as scarlet as Ed.

'What sort of sweets?' I relaxed the tiniest amount, still wondering whether I should go to meet Reg.

'I couldn't tell you,' said Ada. 'It was a plain box with nothing left inside. Tamar's out for the count. I'll get fresh tea.'

She left the room. Connie sat next to me with a face full of concern and sympathy.

'This is not the best time to turn up to talk about the case, is it?'

I kissed Ed's head and heaved a sigh. 'It seems like there'll never be a good moment. Besides —' I cast my eyes upwards in the general direction of Tamar's room, 'it appears the case is following me home anyway. What's happened?'

Connie smoothed Ed's hot curls. 'I came early to tell you that Mr Maynard telephoned the office earlier and spoke to Reg.'

'Is he checking up on us already?'

Connie shook her head. 'Not precisely. Reg thinks he'd sent a newspaper cutting but wasn't sure. The cutting said a wagon team had fallen seriously ill after their load of containers was damaged on the way to various factories, including Fraser's. Some contents were more toxic than others.'

I frowned. 'Was he telephoning from the Department?'

'No idea,' said Connie. 'Reg says Mr Maynard only said he must have got the wrong number. "Must have mislaid the right one. Funny how things disappear, isn't it? Still, no-one dead. Yet." And then he rang off.'

'Whatever did he mean?'

'Reg thought was something to do with the cutting and did a bit of digging in a later edition of the paper. One of the broken containers couldn't be accounted for. It was "cleared" away when the men were being seen to. It wasn't known where it had been destined for, but Mr Maynard clearly thinks it was going to Fraser's.'

'Oh Connie, what shall I do? I want to go to the office, but I can't while Ed's so poorly.'

'Don't fret,' she repeated.

'I'm trying not to. I-I've decided not to get a nanny, Connie. The only applicant who seemed remotely desirable wanted to nurture the elemental something or other.'

'Goodness.'

'Though she called him a sweet little boy which was nice. Oh!' I sat up. Ed, who'd fallen asleep, grumbled a little and then settled down.

'What?' said Connie.

'I've just remembered,' I answered. 'I didn't say it was a boy in the advertisement. I didn't even say how old he was. How did she know?'

CHAPTER 13
Connie

Katherine looked at me for reassurance, for an explanation, and I couldn't help at all.

'I'm sorry, Katherine,' I said. 'Someone knows we're investigating the Crystal Kisses and they want us to stop. It's the only explanation.'

'If I'd known what we'd be getting into when we agreed to take on this "little case", I would never have said yes.' Her green eyes flashed with anger.

'I know.' I met her eyes. 'But don't you want to find out what's behind all this? Don't you want to stop it?'

'I could wring their necks,' Katherine said, quietly, so as not to disturb Ed, and it was worse than if she had shouted the words. 'How *dare* they?'

'Because they're scared,' I said. 'They know we're on their trail.'

'No new staff,' said Katherine decisively. 'Not for either

of us. No going out without telling someone where we're going, and when we'll be back.' She kissed Ed's hot, damp little head. 'Are you sure he's teething?'

I felt Ed's forehead, and peered at his bright red cheeks. 'I'm not a doctor, but it looks like it.'

Slowly, Katherine's shoulders lowered. 'All right. I'll hand him back to Gwen and see what the doctor thinks when she comes. Let's go and see what Tamar has to say for herself.'

***

Poor Tamar didn't have much to say at all, barely managing to croak 'Come in' to Katherine's tap at the door. We found her huddled under the covers, shivering though she was still fully-clothed. She hadn't even bothered to take her cap off. An earthenware bowl, mercifully empty, stood on her bedside table.

'Now, Tamar,' said Katherine, 'whatever have you been doing to get in such a state?'

The covers lowered slightly, and a red, bleary eye peeped out at us. 'Oh, ma'am,' she whimpered, 'I never felt so poorly in my whole life.'

'Ada said you ate some sweets,' Katherine observed, sitting on the bed. 'I take it they didn't agree with you.'

Tamar shook her head, then groaned. 'It feels like my brain's coming loose. Everything hurts.'

'Where did they come from?' asked Katherine. 'Did your young man send them to you?'

The covers moved down a little more, and two red eyes watched us.

'Tamar, I must know where the sweets came from. If

there was something bad in them —'

'It isn't that,' she said, all in a rush. 'I — I ate too many. There's nothing wrong with them, not at all.'

'So it won't hurt to tell me where you got them, will it?'

Tamar blinked. She had clearly never experienced Katherine's persistence before. 'I was sent 'em,' she ventured.

'By whom?'

The bedcovers shrugged.

'Does that mean you don't know?' Katherine waited.

I had to strain my ears to catch Tamar's reply. 'I was sent 'em to try.'

Katherine rolled her eyes at me. 'By whom?'

'The makers.' Another pause. 'It's a club. You pay a bit to join and then they send sweets to taste, and you fill in a card to say what you think, and if they make the sweets for real, you get money for helping.'

'Ahh,' I said. 'Is that your investment, Tamar?'

'It's one of 'em,' she said, as if she had a stock portfolio under the mattress.

'And what did you think of the sweets?'

A weak smile. 'They was lovely,' she said. 'Like strawberries an' cream on a summer day. Till they turned my guts inside out.'

I smiled back. 'I hope you wrote that on the card.'

Tamar just about managed a grin. 'Haven't sent it back yet. Been busy.'

I surveyed the room. A plain postcard was propped on the mantelpiece. 'Is that it, there?' I asked.

Tamar's gaze followed my finger, and she nodded. I

fetched the card, and took my fountain pen from my bag. 'Shall we do it now?'

The card was pre-printed, with a series of boxes to tick. The only handwritten part was the numbers written in the top left-hand corner: *205 and 27B*. 'The top number's how they know it's from me,' said Tamar. 'Dunno what the second number is, it changes every time.'

'*The sweets tasted...*' I read. 'What do you want me to tick, Tamar? I have a choice of *wonderful, nice, all right, not very nice, horrible.*'

'They tasted lovely,' said Tamar. 'So wonderful, I suppose.'

'Done. Next one: *After eating them, I felt...* And it's the same options again.'

''Orrible,' said Tamar, immediately.

'Done. Next statement: *I would buy these sweets if I saw them in a shop.*'

'No,' said Tamar, promptly. 'And no, I wouldn't recommend 'em to a friend, neither. Not if I wanted to keep 'em.'

'All done,' I said, ticking accordingly. 'Do you need a stamp?'

'No, it's got one on,' said Tamar.

I turned the card over. 'So it has.' The card was addressed to *Tester Feedback, PO Box 99, Bermondsey, London.* 'I shall post it for you, Tamar, as I don't imagine you'll be on your feet today.'

'No, ma'am,' Tamar mumbled. 'I'll be up and about tomorrow,' she added hastily, glancing at Katherine.

'Make sure you are,' Katherine replied. 'I'll get the

doctor to examine you when she comes.'

'Don't need a doctor,' muttered Tamar, sulkily.

'Mm.' Katherine rose, looking at the rumpled covers and Tamar's red eyes. 'In my opinion, you do. And if you wish to remain in my employ, you'll listen.' And she left without another word.

***

Once Dr Nicholls had confirmed that Ed was almost certainly teething, and had prescribed foul-tasting medicine for Tamar, we set out for the office. We found Reg aiming a ball of paper at the wastebasket, which was surrounded by failed attempts.

'Keeping busy, Reg?' I asked, and fished the postcard from my bag.

'Oo, what's that?' he said.

'A job for you,' I replied, smiling. 'I want you to see if you can track down who's behind this PO box.' I handed him the card.

'Bermondsey, eh?' he said, scrutinising it. 'Best get changed, then.' He wrinkled his nose.

'And look after yourself, Reg,' said Katherine. 'These people will stop at nothing.'

Reg's brow furrowed. 'D'you think it's the same lot, Miss C?'

Katherine's face became grim. 'I'm sure of it. But I want proof.'

Reg stood up and saluted. 'Right you are, Miss C. I'll do my best. Oh, and a telegram came. I'd have opened it but it was addressed to you, not the agency.' He pointed to a yellow envelope on top of Katherine's in-tray.

'What now?' Katherine muttered, picking it up and ripping it open. 'Cheek!' she exclaimed, and read aloud. *'Get yourselves down here sharpish STOP Sweets deal stopped STOP S still off and no replacement STOP Templeton.'*

We exchanged glances. 'But we'll go, won't we?' I said.

The corner of Katherine's mouth lifted. 'Of course we shall.'

***

'It came in the post this morning,' said Mr Templeton, stabbing a finger at the sheet of sugar-pink paper occupying the centre of his desk, then turning it round for us to read.

NOTICE OF TERMINATION

As you have breached the terms of the agreement it is hereby terminated, and your previous delivery of Crystal Kisses will be your last.

The 'Crystal Kisses' song is the property of, and licensed to, Fraser's Confectionery, and you are no longer permitted to perform it at your music hall.

The name 'Crystal Kisses' is a registered trademark. You may not use it in any new work without permission from Fraser's, which, regrettably, we must withhold.

Thank you for your cooperation in this matter.

Yours sincerely,

A. Sweet, for Fraser's Confectionery.

'Short and not very sweet,' I observed. 'But what do you want us to do about it?'

Mr Templeton goggled at me, then rolled his eyes at an imaginary audience. 'Waddaya think? I want you to find out who's behind this muck and take 'em down, that's what.'

Katherine grinned. 'You've changed your tune, Mr T.'

'Yes, I 'ave,' he said, wagging a finger at her. 'I thought it was too good to be true, and by God I was right. An' now I want you to fix it. Ellen's still singing, thank the Lord, but none of her songs are a draw like that Crystal Kisses one was. An' Selina's still on the sick list, so I'm a dancer and a fake medium down an' all.'

'So am I right in thinking you expect us to make up the deficiencies in your playbill *and* unmask whatever villainy might be going on with the Crystal Kisses?' said Katherine.

Mr Templeton shrugged. 'Wouldn't hurt. Whatever you do, make it funny. Dan Datchett's comic song about bickering in the Balkans was so bad it had the punters throwing things. Revenge is one thing, business is another.'

Katherine raised her eyebrows at me. I considered, and nodded. 'All right,' she said. 'We shall, but we'll need your cooperation.'

Mr Templeton stretched a large, gnarled hand across the desk. 'Then you got it,' he said.

***

'I don't understand,' I said, as the cab took us out of Lambeth and into an unexpectedly nice area. 'I was sure there was a spy among the music-hall staff, but Mr Templeton hasn't taken on anyone new in the last month. Unless you count us.'

'I know,' said Katherine, as the cab slowed down. 'I think this is it,' she said doubtfully, as we stopped outside a block of mansion flats. She pressed the button for 31A and two minutes later we saw Ellen's small figure through the glass.

'Fancy,' she said without emotion, as she let us in. 'Come to visit the patient, 'ave we?'

'We have,' said Katherine. 'And to talk to you.'

She sniffed. 'I wondered 'ow long it'd be before old Templeton dragged you back in. I still ain't singing that song.' She led the way upstairs. 'There ain't any too much time to chat, though, I must get going myself in an hour or so.'

Selina lay in a clean white bed, looking like death. 'Afternoon,' she croaked.

'I'm sorry you aren't any better,' I said, taking her hand.

'Better than I was,' she said.

'Do you feel sick?' asked Katherine, and I thought of the earthenware bowl next to Tamar.

Selina shook her head. 'Just — achy all over, and hot. And tired, but I can't sleep. And my teeth hurt.' A feeble smile. 'Too many sweets.'

'I wouldn't be surprised.' Katherine smoothed her hair back from her forehead. 'She's very warm,' she said to me. 'It isn't the same thing.'

'The same thing as what?' asked Ellen, sharply.

Katherine turned to her. 'One of my maids binged on some sweets; apparently she's a taster on the side. She was sick, and shivery, and had a bad headache. Selina's symptoms are entirely different.'

'We don't know that they're the same sweets,' I said. 'Besides, the lab analysis said there was nothing much in the Crystal Kisses except sugar and caffeine.'

'Then why do I feel so rough?' asked Selina, and a tear trickled onto the pillow.

'I don't know,' said Katherine, stroking her hair. 'But we're going to find out, and hopefully make you better.' Her other hand clenched into a fist. 'And make sure this doesn't happen to anyone else, ever again.'

CHAPTER 14
Katherine

We had less than twenty-four hours in which to come up with something for Friday and Saturday's performances at the Merrymakers which would keep the crowds happy. It didn't seem long enough. Connie and I had to make peace with our respective families before we could go back on stage.

'Do you remember when we thought our freedom was only impeded by your mother and my Aunt Alice?' I said, as we made our way to Joyce Square.

Connie sighed. 'We thought that without their control, we could do whatever we liked.'

'I felt guilty once,' I remembered. 'The night Aunt Alice thought I'd been murdered. Apart from that, it was just annoying and I couldn't wait to be independent. Now…'

'Now you feel neglectful.'

'Yes. Perhaps we could bring the children and put them on the stage instead of us.' I chuckled, imagining the chaos as our trio of children, painted and organised by Bee, marched around in the spotlights.

'My word,' said Connie. 'Poor Mr Templeton would have a heart attack.' The cab rattled to a halt outside my house. Connie gave me a worn-out smile which I suspected was reflected in my face, and squeezed my hand. 'Hopefully one of us will have some sensible idea in the morning. Do you suppose Tina will help?'

I gave her a hug. 'I don't know,' I said as I opened the cab door. 'She won't do anything she doesn't want to.' I yawned. 'Oh, I'll be so glad to see James. See you tomorrow bright and early.'

***

I managed 'early' the following morning. 'Bright' was impossible.

'Gor,' said Reg as I removed my hat. 'Wot you bin doing, Miss C? Sleeping in an 'edge?'

I put my hand up to my hair as I stared into the mirror. On one side of my head the pins had come loose; over my left ear untamed curls billowed in chaos, while over the right, they lay neatly restrained. Connie approached with a brush and tutted.

'More to the point,' she said, helping me re-dress my hair and indicating the shadows under my eyes, 'did you sleep at all? Or have you been practising a new make-up technique? I'm assuming Ed kept you awake.'

I groaned through a yawn, wincing a little as Connie caught a tangle. 'He is most definitely teething — started howling at midnight and didn't stop till six. The whole household took it in turns to try and comfort him. Apart from Tamar, of course. I'm hoping that listening to a wailing baby might make her more careful about what she gets up to with her young man. Margaret was the one who finally got him to settle. They're both still curled up on the sofa, fast asleep. I think I've had about three hours —' My words disappeared into another yawn.

'Did James help too?' Connie rammed the last pin in with enough force to keep an elephant tethered. My brain rattled. 'I hope he doesn't doze off when he gets to the factory.'

'He didn't come home yesterday.' I patted my bruised head and went to see if the tea was fresh.

'What? Why? Is he all right? Where —'

'Morning all.' Connie's flood of questions was interrupted by Tina entering with a letter in her hand. 'I intercepted the postman,' she said. 'I thought I'd save his legs.'

It was a cheap envelope addressed to me with a familiar scrawl and postmarked 7 a.m. She exchanged it for the teapot which was tipping in my tired hands. 'I'll make another pot, shall I? Or should we take you for coffee? You look done in.'

'I'll be fine,' I said, slitting open the letter. 'As long as no-one cries. I'm not sure my nerves could stand it. Just prod me if I start to snooze.'

'Yes, but James,' persisted Connie. 'How can you be so calm about him?'

I waved the letter at her. 'Because he's all right. Do you

remember I told you the *Voice* owns a small house in Clerkenwell which they use as a safe house?'

'Yes, you did,' said Connie. 'The one which reporters sometimes use when they go undercover?'

'That's right,' I said. 'James gave it as his address when he applied for the job. He got a message to me last night to say he thought he'd stay there, in case anyone checked. At two a.m., when I was padding up and down the landing with Ed, I had a good mind to go and join him. Let's see what he has to say.'

The letter was, for James, rather restrained. All the same I decided not to declare the opening lines which read *To My Music-Hall Princess of the Emerald Dress, How may I compare thee to a silken frog? Hope Ed is taking his role as head of the house seriously and keeping all you women under control. (Poor chap.) There are two reporters and a bloke from the Isle of Dogs bunking down here and I'm surprised the roof is still on — they snore worse than you.*

I cleared my throat and hoped that was the last of the personal messages as everyone waited for me to read aloud.

Everyone in the office is very conscientious. Pearson the chief clerk appears a pleasant man and had me typing invoices today — mainly to small shops and one or two family-run hotels. Someone else gave me the details on a long sheet of paper. I'd expected to be handed the ledger and go from there. Several people do the same task, only from different sheets. It feels as if everyone works on just one thing.

A more important set of persons open letters received and share them out. Someone deals with requests for business. Someone else with advertising. Someone ticks off receipts of money against the lists and hands them to a much more important person. The ledger-keeper checks everything — goods out, invoices out, monies in etc — and the ledger is then taken by Pearson to be locked away. It's an impressive beast, about two feet by one and three inches thick, with a tooled cover and marbling on the page edges. I'm sure it's equally impressive inside, but I couldn't see.

'Sounds worse than the Department,' said Reg. 'I never thought I'd see another place which could make a simple job unnecessarily complicated.'

I asked if I could see into the factory itself. 'Of course,' said Pearson. 'I'm sure Stone won't mind.'

Stone, who's the foreman, did mind, however. He thought I might put the sugar off the boil or the men off their stroke or something. 'Education don't make you intelligent,' Stone said. 'The last pen-pusher who came and looked asked if the mixture was hot, and put his hand in before we could answer. Fool. He'll never use that hand again. We haven't let a clerk in since.' What I did find out, though, is that the packing line is entirely female. If you're missing me, perhaps you could apply!

I asked Pearson if staff can get Crystal Kisses at a lower price and he seemed aghast. 'Absolutely not,' he said, and then he changed tack. 'That's to say, everyone is sick of them after a week or so of working here — same as any factory. By the way, I'm impressed with your work, I might have something different for you tomorrow.'

I yawned and let the letter droop.

'That's strange,' said Connie, handing me a cup of tea. 'You'd think they'd keep him on one job for at least a week, so he could get used to it.'

'Mmm,' said Tina. 'Unless they don't want him memorising the addresses.'

'Could be,' Reg pondered. 'Although it's probably too late. Didn't you once say Mr King's good at remembering anything he's read? Does he say what they want him to do next? I hope it's the advertising contacts. I could do with some help.'

I picked up the letter again and gasped.

'What?' everyone said together.

My new task tomorrow is to prepare cards. Pearson showed me an example. It has a set of questions about what a customer likes or doesn't like about Crystal Kisses. I'll have to number a new set from numbers on another sheet and batch them up with samples. It sounds deadly dull. Before I could read through it properly a bell went and we were all sent to get lunch.

I got back a little earlier than the others and overheard Pearson talking on the telephone. 'Too strong? We need to tone them down and build it up slowly. The cards to Birm —' Then the lunch-time bell in the factory rang and drowned out the rest, not to mention the fact that the other clerks were coming up the stairs.

I'll write again this evening. Hope you're not planning any ill-considered gallivanting nor wearing any more stupid dresses. But if you are — stay safe because I love you.

I read the last two sentences before I realised what they said, and felt myself blush as the others cleared their throats and grinned.

'Birm?' asked Tina, looking over my shoulder. 'What do you think that is? Birmingham?'

I shrugged.

'Honestly, Katherine,' said Connie. 'You really do need sleep. James only heard the beginning of the word so probably assumed Birmingham. It must be to do with Bermondsey — where the cards are being received.'

'Yeah,' said Reg. '"The cards to Bermondsey report customers say Crystal Kisses make them chuck" or something. I didn't get too far yesterday evening, but I'll have another pop today while I'm hunting down the printers.'

'What have I missed this time?' said Tina.

'It's a long story,' I told her, putting my elbows on the desk and my chin in my hands. The desk looked very inviting. 'Connie can explain it a minute, but we need to ask you a favour first. Would you —'

'Do another stint at the music hall?'

'How did you guess?'

Tina tapped her temple and grinned. 'I'm a clairvoyant,

aren't I? Anyway, it was fun. Mr Hamilton pretends to be a bit put out but he doesn't mind really. It's not like anyone knows it's me. But what about you two? You'll never get away with that song again.'

'We're not going to try,' said Connie. 'Mr Templeton has been told in no uncertain terms he can't use the tune or the name. I still think there's someone at the theatre who's involved, and we can work it out if we're there. If you do your act that's one draw for the public, but Katherine and I must do something else. If only we could come up with an idea…'

'If only I had more energy,' I said, lifting my head off the desk and stifling a yawn.

'That's it!' cried Connie, pulling a notepad towards her and picking up her pencil. 'Katherine, you're a genius.'

'Am I?' I asked.

'Oh yes,' Connie replied. 'A *suffering* genius.' She grinned.

'Ohhh…' I picked up a pencil of my own and went to sit beside her. 'Now, how does it go?'

Chapter 15
Connie

'That,' I said, grinning at the two sheets of notebook paper covered with my scribbles and Katherine's, 'will do nicely. Reg, can you type up two copies for us, please?'

Reg took the sheets, scanned them, and snorted. 'If you get away with that...' Then he eyed Katherine. 'If you don't mind me asking, how are you gonna...?'

Katherine beamed. 'You'll see.'

Reg fed a new sheet of paper into the typewriter, and was squaring up to the task when the telephone rang. 'Caster and Fleet Agency,' he said, in his best office tones, then listened. 'May I ask who is calling, please?' He covered the mouthpiece with his hand and gave me a significant look. 'It's yer ma.'

My eyebrows shot up. 'Mother?' I bounced out of my seat and took the receiver. 'Mother, is that you?'

'Didn't the nice young man say?' Mother replied, with

extremely clear diction.

'Are you all right? Is Father well? Has something happened?'

'Do calm yourself, Connie,' she said, with a tinkling laugh. 'Nothing is wrong. I merely telephoned to ask if you would like to accompany me to an invitation-only viewing of Mr Landy's new painting this afternoon at the Lansdowne Gallery. Your father has excused himself.'

My brain whirred. Frederick Landy was an artist specialising in depictions of pretty children and small dogs. I had never known my mother to enter an art gallery.

'I am waiting, Connie.' I sensed a *Constance* in her tone.

'Um, yes, I could,' I said. 'What time?' I pictured myself dashing to the Merrymakers and running into the wings to sing for Katherine.

'The picture will be unveiled at two o'clock.'

I heaved a sigh of relief. 'Wonderful. I'll meet you there at a quarter to. I'd love to chat, Mother, but I'm in the middle of something. We'll talk at the gallery.'

'Indeed. Goodbye, dear.' And the connection ended.

I put the telephone down to see Katherine staring at me. 'You're going to view Frederick Landy's latest painting with your mother?'

'I'll take the song with me and practise in the carriage,' I gabbled. 'Don't worry, I'll make sure I leave by three and I'll go straight to the Merrymakers.' Then I saw her expression. 'You don't mind, then?'

'Mind?' Her grin broadened. 'You have access to the latest painting by an artist whose work is regularly bought to advertise things from soap to sweets? Of course I don't mind!' Then her grin was replaced by a businesslike look. 'Let's discuss the song list before you go.'

***

I arrived at the gallery at a quarter to two precisely to find Mother's carriage already outside, managing somehow to look impatient.

'There you are, dear,' said Mother, as I approached the window. 'I did wonder.'

I sighed inwardly, and waited while Hodgkins handed her out, then waited while she brushed an invisible speck from her glove and made sure her hat was on straight. 'Do come along,' she said, and marched into the gallery, ignoring the bow of the commissionaire completely.

'Mrs Swift!' A tall, energetic man, presumably the gallery owner, was at her side in a moment. 'How marvellous to see you. And this is…?'

'This is my daughter, Mrs Lamont,' said Mother, in tones which, though not loud, were clear enough to carry throughout the large room.

'It is indeed a pleasure,' said the man, bouncing to my side and offering a hand. 'I am Jacob Smallbone, ma'am, proprietor of the Lansdowne Gallery. Let me introduce you both to the artist.'

He led us towards a man in a brown velvet suit, standing in front of a shrouded picture and gazing at it as if he could see the painting beneath. 'Mr Landy, two of your admirers.'

The man turned. He was heavily bearded, with long shaggy hair, but I saw a distinct twinkle in his eye. 'At least you're not going to use my creative talents to sell dish soap. Or are you?'

Mother drew back a little. 'I should hope not.'

'In that case, I am glad to meet you.' He shook hands with both Mother and me, his grip firm and purposeful.

'But you don't have to sell your paintings to people who do that,' I said, smiling.

The twinkle again. 'Touché, Miss —'

'Mrs Lamont.'

'And you're right. Strictly speaking, I don't. But if I want to live to a decent standard, and support my family, and have money to buy more paint and canvases, then —'

'Landy!' A short broad man with a shock of white hair and heavy side-whiskers clapped him on the arm and pumped his hand up and down. 'Tantalising us, eh? What have you dreamt up this time?'

'Mr Fraser,' said Mr Landy, and while his voice was easy, his shoulders had stiffened. 'Always a pleasure.'

Fraser... I gazed at the man, who was perhaps in his sixties, plainly dressed but in materials which suggested his status. Could this bluff man hold the key to the Crystal Kisses?

A little bell rang, followed by Mr Smallbone clearing his throat. 'It is time, everyone, please take your places.' He began shooing people towards the painting. There were perhaps thirty people there, and Mother and I were the only women.

Mr Landy freed himself from Mr Fraser's grip, and sauntered over to the black hangings. 'Good afternoon, everyone. Lovely to see you all.' He grinned. 'I won't keep you waiting.' He grasped the edge of the black drapery with both hands, and flung it up as if he were shaking a tablecloth. '*Child's Play.*'

'Ooo,' cooed the audience.

The painting showed three little girls, their hands joined, playing ring-a-ring-o'-roses in a meadow. The sky was blue, the grass green, the girls' expressions joyful. But what struck me most of all was the colour of each girl's silk dress — one red, one yellow, and one green — and how it exactly matched the colours of a bag of Crystal Kisses.

Mr Fraser sidled up to the artist and muttered in his ear. Mr Landy nodded, and eyed the rest of the audience. Two men conferred across the room from me, but the taller of the two was shaking his head. Another man, rather nervous, walked up and leaning in, murmured to the artist, who looked politely interested. Two more drifted up, glancing at Mr Fraser as they did so, but they seemed defeated before they even began. I glanced at Mother, who was eyeing the painting with something like contempt.

Mr Landy took Mr Smallbone aside, and it was no surprise when the little bell tinkled again. 'I am delighted to announce that *Child's Play* has been bought by Mr Fraser.' I noticed a man scribbling in a notebook — a reporter, I assumed — and made a note to check the papers tomorrow morning. 'May I?' He indicated the painting, and the cloth.

'Leave it another ten minutes,' chuckled Mr Fraser. 'They'll be seeing plenty of it in the future.' He slung an arm round the artist's shoulders, and led him away.

The crowd, either thwarted or bored, dispersed rapidly, until only Mother and I were standing before the painting.

'Well, that's that,' she said, checking herself for signs of scruffiness which might have materialised in the last twenty minutes.

'Mother...'

She picked a loose thread from her sleeve. 'Yes, dear?'

'Why did you have tickets for the viewing? I didn't know you liked art.'

Her mouth tightened. 'I don't, dear. However, one must do something, and it is preferable to sales of work.' She swept out, and I had no choice but to follow in her wake.

***

'How do I look?' asked Katherine, twirling and grinning.

I shuddered. 'Terrible.'

'You look like some sort of clown,' added Linnie, smirking. 'I'm glad I don't have to make such a guy of myself.'

'Thank you,' Katherine replied. 'But who's top of the bill?'

Katherine had stuck to one of her usual outrageously-colourful Felicity outfits for the first half, with her hair loose at the back. Now, though, she had painted purple shadows under her eyes, and brushed up her hair until it stuck out all around her head in an auburn frizz.

'You'll regret that later,' I said, picking up a strand, which crackled with energy.

Katherine shrugged. 'So long as it does the trick.' She grinned at me again.

'Please don't do that,' I said, and headed for the wings with my song-sheet.

Reg was by the side of the stage and winked at me. 'All right?' I mouthed.

He grinned and stuck up two thumbs. I took a deep breath and studied the words for the hundredth time, though they danced before my eyes.

The dancers, still minus Selina, took a last curtain call and tripped off the stage, while Mr Templeton walked on, applauding them. 'Loverly, girls, loverly,' he said. 'Now where's my favourite songbird?'

He waited. The audience waited. And Katherine ran on stage, falling over her feet. 'Right here, Mr Templeton sir!' She clicked her heels, saluted, and almost toppled.

''Old up, 'old up, Felicity,' he said, taking her by the elbows. 'Are you all right?'

'Of course I am!' said Katherine, breaking free and capering round the stage. 'I've just had a wonderful tonic!'

'You don't look wonderful,' said Mr Templeton, scratching his head.

'No she doesn't!' shouted a man in the audience.

'You be quiet!' Katherine shouted back, putting her hands on her hips and peering past the lights. 'I've had my sweeties and I'm ready for anything!'

'Ready for anything?' said Mr Templeton, and the band struck up.

'Oh yes!' Katherine faced the audience, opened her mouth, and I sang.

'I bought some lovely sweeties,

They're tasty as can be,
My friends all eat 'em, yes they do,
It isn't only me.
They said they'd keep me going,
And well, what do you think?
I danced all night, and then I found
I couldn't sleep a wink!'

While Katherine pretended to rub her eyes and yawn between verses, I peered into the audience. I saw grins, and tapping feet. I gave a thumbs-up to Katherine, who continued.

'I bought some lovely sweeties
And ate them in one go,
That's how I learnt my lesson that
You need to take 'em slow.
They make you go for hours,
They're dainty things to munch.
The only thing about 'em is
They make you lose your lunch!'

Katherine rubbed her stomach with a pained expression and mimed being sick, and the audience roared with laughter.

'I bought some lovely sweeties
And then I wanted more,
I spent all of my money,
And ate 'em by the score.

They give you lots of energy,
Of that there is no doubt —
The only thing about 'em is
They make your teeth fall out!'

Katherine grinned hugely at the audience, who recoiled — and well they might, for Ellen and I had covered every other front tooth with black court-plaster. 'Let my dreadful plight be a warning to you!' she called, and twirled off stage to my side of the wings.

The audience were applauding and stamping their feet. 'Sing it again!' someone shouted. 'Never a truer word!' The stamping increased.

Katherine raised her eyebrows at me, and I nodded. She stuck her head out of the wings. 'Again? You want me to tell you this tale of woe and suffering *again*?'

'YES!' bellowed the audience.

Mr Templeton's grin nearly split his head in two. 'You heard 'em, Felicity,' he roared. 'Get yourself out here!'

Katherine put on an exasperated face. 'Oh very *well*,' she said, and danced into the lights.

CHAPTER 16
Katherine

I felt flat when I arrived home, and the house was echoey and cold.

The afternoon post had brought a letter from James's sister Evangeline, now Mrs Maurice Lamont, begging me to visit. She was in the last stages of pregnancy and desperate for someone to distract her mother from worrying over her every move. Unable to go myself, I sent Ed and Gwen with Margaret instead. They would be more than enough distraction to give Evangeline the peace she needed: Ed would be indulged to his heart's content, Gwen could get some rest, and Margaret could 'observe' the young country doctor with whom she had a lopsided correspondence.

I found Ada in the kitchen and she made us both cocoa. 'How is Tamar?' I asked.

Ada's lips narrowed. 'Perfectly well, if you ask me.

She's in bed now, of course, and I daresay she's rotting her mind with a romantic novel. You should never have put electricity in the maids' bedrooms.' She took a sip of cocoa, shook her head and added a spoonful of sugar.

'She's entitled to rest,' I pointed out. 'Susan's in her room too, isn't she? And we're all exhausted from Ed's teething shenanigans.'

Ada made an incoherent noise. Rest, in her view, was a necessary but regrettable waste of life. 'You should have sent Tamar to the country too,' she said.

'I could only send so many people to Hazelgrove. Even *my* mother-in-law has a limit to her fussing abilities.'

'Her young man is a worry.' Ada's words confused me until I realised she was talking about Tamar.

'Has he visited today?'

'Yes,' said Ada. 'She'd got word to him and he wanted to see her in her sick bed. The very idea. I told him anyone who could put away as much food as she did today was fit enough to catch up her duties and that's what she'd be doing, and he could take his gifts and wait for her day off unless he wanted her dismissed.' Ada looked at me, her face puzzled. 'Mrs Kitty — why have you still got a snood over your hair?'

I raised my hand and pulled it off. My hair exploded like a chrysanthemum. 'Erm,' I said. 'I need your help.'

***

Very early the following morning I smoothed down the grey stuff dress I kept for going incognito and fixed a simple black hat to my sore head. I was reasonably sure that Ada had pulled out sufficient tangled hair to stuff a cushion but it had still been a struggle to tame the remainder and put it up in a neat style.

Now she helped me into a cloak and gave me the appraisal she saved for when she was more worried than usual. It resembled indigestion. 'Are you sure you'll be safe, Mrs Kitty?'

'It's all quite respectable,' I reminded her. 'If I'm not home for tea, get word to Connie.' I left the house and walked to the tube.

An hour later I was at Fraser's factory, trying to control the shake in my hands as I was timed to see how fast I could sort and box and tie ribbons.

'That'll do,' the foreman said after five minutes which felt like a year. 'You can have a trial run till lunch-time and if you do well, you can start on Monday. We offer half-days you understand, morning or afternoon. Afternoons are for the experienced women.'

'Yes, sir.'

'And female staff are prohibited from fraternising with any of the men, so don't get up hopes of matrimony. Right then, follow me.'

If I'd thought typing and housework were monotonous, it was because I hadn't understood the repetition of a factory. The sweets came in huge batches put on a long table, and a first set of women checked each individually at a speed which would have made my eyes water if I'd had time to watch. They placed these in two containers. The first was passed to a table which sorted them into jars for shops. The second was tipped onto our table, where we sorted them into boxes with so many of each colour. The boxes were nothing like the one described by Tamar. They were printed with the name *Fraser's* at a diagonal and a picture of a nauseating little boy in blue velvet kissing an equally nauseating little girl with rosy cheeks. A fourth table checked the contents of the boxes and tied a neat ribbon round them. After two hours, we had a break for tea which we took from an urn before stretching our legs in the yard. The men from the manufacturing section had just gone indoors and the clerks, I knew from James, were served tea in the office. I glanced up to where I assumed he was and took in the narrow outer gallery and the smeared windows. The air in the yard was sticky with fumes and heat oozing from the boiling-room. I rolled my shoulders and stretched. I had never ached so much in my life.

I smiled at my fellow workers, who smiled in return. They seemed chatty enough, although still weighing me up a little. One of them, however, as we went inside, whispered, 'It's nice here, it ain't good to do so much staring.'

Two hours later, the shift was over. Worn out, I collected up my things and reported to the foreman. 'You'll do for the time being, seeing as we're short,' he said. 'Come back Monday morning. But you won't stay unless you speed up. And mind what I say about the men. Especially the clerks. Don't think they're a leg up, they're more likely to take advantage.'

When, as I left the factory, a nice-looking man coming from a different door fell into step and tried to address me, I remembered what the foreman had said, lifted my head and increased my pace, leaving him to fall behind. No-one could accuse me of being fraternised with. Even by my own husband.

***

'I'm glad you had the sense to wear a wig tonight,' said Connie as we waited to be served a late supper after our performance at the Merrymakers. She touched her eyebrow as a sign I should check mine and, feeling sorry for the laundry maid, I left a remnant of lurid make-up on Simpson's best table linen.

'What did she do last night?' queried James. With the help of Reg and a press colleague, he had changed from down-at-heel junior clerk to his normal smart self, and we would be together until Monday morning.

'Don't ask,' I said.

Albert snorted. 'If you imagine a dandelion on fire, you'd get the idea.'

James gave a mirthless laugh. 'That's a dangerous song you're singing.'

'That's the idea,' said Connie. 'We want to flush them out. I went to see Selina this morning while Katherine was tying pretty ribbons.'

'I don't think I'd be trusted with that yet,' I admitted, sipping my wine.

'Having seen the way you do your plaits…' Connie gave me a grin, but like James's there was little humour behind it.

'How is Selina?' asked Albert.

'Getting better.' Connie paused as chicken in a cream sauce was placed before her. 'The doctor was there too. He says she can return to work on Monday provided she isn't too energetic.'

'What did he say had caused the illness?'

'He wasn't sure,' said Connie. 'He said he'd seen something like it, but this couldn't have come from eating sweets.'

'I just can't find any evidence in the factory,' said James. 'I mean, there might be information in one of the ledgers, but I only managed to see them being taken out once by dropping a bottle of ink right by the doorway. That was docked from my wages. I tried to memorise the combination for the safe and can't be sure without trying whether I had it right or not. There's certainly something I'm not being allowed to do — yet. And there was nothing obvious on the packing floor?'

'I've only been there a morning,' I pointed out. 'It's funny about the shifts, though. Unusual not to do a whole day in a factory, surely? Not that I *could* do that, of course. I went to get a feel of the place but I'll go back on Monday and see if anyone talks to me.'

'It'll be very general if they're like the clerks,' said James. 'No-one seemed interested that I was visiting my old mother,' he gave me a wink, 'or asked where she lived. They talk about sport mostly, though betting is frowned upon by management. Oh, and the savings club. I haven't been there long enough to have it explained to me. I've still to see the actual manufacture of the sweets or the raw ingredient orders. I only got to peek at the ledgers because Pearson was talking to Stone about one of the drivers. "Still in the infirmary," Stone said. "That powder's terrible stuff."'

'Powdered sugar?' mused Albert.

James shrugged and continued. 'Then Pearson said, "What about the horses?" And the foreman said, "Never mind the horses."'

Connie put her knife and fork down.

Albert scanned us all. 'Connie — I know you don't want my opinion, but I think you should stop. This is a job for the police.'

James and I looked at each other and then at Connie and Albert. Connie seemed as exhausted as I felt. I knew we were all thinking of our children, tucked up fast asleep under warm covers and it was so tempting to say we should give up… But then I thought of Selina and Tamar and all the people slowly being ensnared by Crystal Kisses, and I knew we couldn't.

'The police would laugh in our faces,' I said. 'We must find out what's happening and why. One more week. Agreed?'

I reached for Connie's hand and she returned my clasp.

'Agreed,' she said.

CHAPTER 17
Connie

Sunday truly was a day of rest. Albert and I both slept late; he generally did on a Sunday, and I was too tired from a double performance at the Merrymakers to think about moving from my bed until nine. I felt shockingly lazy; but when I saw myself in the dressing-table mirror, still drawn even after a good night's sleep, I knew that a day off was in order. So we took the children to the park, I read a silly novel, we dined well, and altogether I had a thoroughly good time. I hoped that Katherine had had the sense to do the same.

My good spirits abated somewhat on Monday morning when I arrived at the office and realised I was on my own. Katherine would be packing at Fraser's till noon, while Reg had left a note for me: *As wagon trail has gone cold, going to try and find the Bermondsey address again. See you later, Reg.*

I sighed, put the kettle on, and fidgeted while it worked its slow way to boiling. The office was tidy; nothing to put away, nothing for my twitching fingers to straighten. The wall was blurred by a rising wisp of steam from the kettle. It recalled Selina dressed as Madame Cravatini, cheerfully prophesying at the music hall while smoke plumed and scarves waved and chaos reigned around her.

On Saturday Selina had remained confined to bed; sitting up, admittedly, and eating well, but she said she was still tired and full of aches. The doctor had arrived while I was there, a nice, bluff, reassuring man. He had listened to her symptoms, taken her pulse, looked in her eyes, watched as she stood up, trembling despite Ellen's supporting arm, and still professed himself puzzled. 'Four days since she collapsed, you say?'

Selina lay there, hands folded on the counterpane, her eyes huge and troubled. 'Don't worry my dear, I'm sure we'll have you right as rain in no time!' he said, and cast a significant glance towards the kitchenette.

Ellen and I followed him, and he half-closed the door. 'She's a performer, you say?'

Ellen nodded. 'Dancer, comedienne, bit of everything. Music hall.'

'Ah, the music hall...' He sounded wistful, as if that were a pleasure now denied him. 'I shall prescribe a tonic, and perhaps getting back to work will perk her up, but no dancing. Her pulse is much quicker than I would like. If she can do her act sitting down, fine.' He looked around as if the walls had ears, and lowered his voice still further. 'I've seen something like this once — much worse — but I can't think how it could have happened from eating sweets.'

'What?' asked Ellen, suspiciously.

'Much worse, you understand,' he murmured. 'And he was a young man, from a good family. Cocaine, injected intravenously. The same rapid heartbeat, fatigue, aches and pains, and toothache from constant grinding. His family called me in, pleaded with me, even considered locking him up for his own good... But the addiction was too strong, and he died of an overdose two months later. However, there is no way that eating sweets, even ones laced with cocaine, could produce anything like the same effect. It's impossible. Hopefully time and care will mend your friend.' He scribbled a few words on his pad, handed it to Ellen in exchange for his fee, and left, his feet surprisingly noiseless.

Ellen and I exchanged glances. 'How can I tell her?' she whispered, her blue eyes wide.

The whistle of the kettle brought me out of my reverie, followed almost immediately by the bang of the office door.

'At least *that's* good timing,' said Katherine, hurrying over and filling the teapot.

'I thought you were at Fraser's this morning,' I said, weakly.

Katherine found another cup and set it down with a clack. She bristled with unspent energy; her clothes rustled, her eyes flashed green.

'I was,' she said. 'Until the gates opened. The foreman made a beeline for me and said they'd found someone who could work faster, so I wouldn't be needed.'

'But you'd only been there a morning.'

'Yes.' Katherine folded her arms and frowned at the teapot. 'I think they guessed I wasn't who I said I was. It's hard to explain.' She scowled. 'A woman told me off for staring. Maybe it was her. Anyway, that avenue's closed now.'

I thought about putting a consoling arm round Katherine, but I suspected I might get an electric shock if I did. 'You didn't come straight here, did you?'

'Don't be ridiculous,' spat Katherine. 'I took two tube lines, doubled back and got in a cab. I'm not a complete fool.'

I poured the tea, feeling it was the best thing I could do under the circumstances. 'Maybe James will turn something up.'

'Maybe,' Katherine said listlessly. Then she cocked her head, like a dog listening. 'Or maybe not,' she said, setting her cup down and going to the door. She opened it and James came into view, dressed in his usual clothes. 'Fancy seeing you here,' she said.

'I could say the same thing to you,' he replied, and gathered her in his arms. 'Got your marching orders?'

Katherine nodded. 'Too slow,' she muttered.

'Ahhh.' James kissed the top of her head. 'I was too careless, apparently, so with regret Fraser's and I have parted company.'

'I'm sorry,' I said, walking over and patting James's shoulder. 'Although I didn't think it was a good career move at the time.'

'No.' He sighed. 'And what's really aggravating is that I don't have enough material for as much as a paragraph.'

'What's really aggravating is that we've both been spotted.' Katherine's grip on James's arm tightened. 'Is that a coincidence?'

'It shows that Fraser's is vigilant,' I said. 'And while I understand that a manufacturer would want to guard some of their methods and recipes, that level of secrecy suggests they have more to hide than most. I wonder…'

Katherine looked at me. 'What, Connie?'

'I wonder if there's another way in. I might telephone Albert. Just let me think about it a bit.'

Katherine sighed. 'You can keep secrets as well as Fraser's, Connie.'

'There is a bright side to all this, of course,' said James, releasing Katherine and fetching himself a cup.

'What's that?' Katherine and I said, simultaneously.

'Well…' He poured himself tea, and grinned at us both. 'At least I don't have to rely on my earnings from the factory, as my wife's alter ego, noted music-hall chanteuse Felicity Velour, can keep me in the manner to which I am accustomed.'

'Oh, she will,' said Katherine, grimly. 'You can rely on her. *Oh!*' Her sudden grin was like sunshine breaking through storm clouds.

'I'm glad you're pleased at the prospect,' said James.

'It isn't that,' she replied. 'When I was waiting for the second tube train I saw a poster for Crystal Kisses, and two people were standing in front of it.'

'Why are you smiling at that?' I asked, thoroughly

perplexed.

Katherine's grin widened. 'They were humming our song!'

***

'Glad you could make it, ladies,' said Mr Templeton, waving us to seats.

'Not a problem, Mr T,' said Katherine breezily. 'Why the rush?'

We had been summoned to the music hall by telegram: *Can you get here for five STOP Got a proposition STOP Maybe bring sandwiches STOP Templeton.*

Mr Templeton eyed us both, then took a cigar from its box and clamped his mouth round it. 'Got an offer to make, ain't I?'

'What sort of offer?' I asked.

He grinned. 'You'll like this, ladies. As you know, word gets around. I got a couple of notes on Saturday, from colleagues in the biz. Apparently some of their friends and neighbours had visited us on Friday, and been bowled over by your song. So they asked if I'd mind renting you out, so to speak.' He chuckled. 'Don't look so worried!'

'And what did you say?' asked Katherine.

'Obviously I said yes. On condition you're back to wrap up the show for me. What I had in mind was, you do your first half songs here, a bit earlier on the bill so Madame C can wrap up the first half an' get to bed.'

'Good,' said Katherine. 'Then what?'

'Then you put on your get-up and travel, by whatever conveyance you wish, to the Jollity, and go on after the next act. Then to the Regal, and so on. I reckon you can get four in plus a little rest before you go on here for the grand finale.'

'You want us to do it *five times*?' said Katherine, rather faintly.

'I know,' said Mr Templeton. 'Wonderful, ain't it?'

'I'm not sure that's what I'd call it,' she replied, with a snort.

'Think about it, though,' Mr Templeton wheedled. 'It's a chance to spread your message a lot wider than if you just stuck here.'

'True...' Katherine seemed to be visualising a pleasant future. Then she turned to me. 'What do you think, Connie?'

'Honestly?' My head was spinning. Evenings of being whirled around in cabs from music hall to music hall, dashing to the wings, and singing the same song over and over, like a musical box... But if it helped to fight the menace of Crystal Kisses... 'If you can manage it, Katherine, I'll do it.'

'I'll do my best,' said Katherine. 'What's in it for us? Apart from our noble cause, of course.'

Mr Templeton looked injured. 'I thought you two were ladies of leisure nowadays.'

'That's as may be,' I said. 'But we still don't come for nothing.'

He grimaced. 'Awright. Half what the other halls are paying me for your services.'

I stretched out a hand. 'Done.'

He shook it with a wide grin. 'That's a relief. You start tonight.'

'*Tonight?*' I gawped at him. 'What about our arrangements?'

'Easy peasy,' he said calmly. 'I'll send Ron with you, he knows all the staff and he'll look after you.'

'I'll go and wire James,' said Katherine. 'Connie, could we take Tredwell and your carriage?'

'We might as well announce our names when we go on stage,' I said. 'I have a better idea. I'll tell you on the way to the telegraph office.'

***

'Are you ready?' asked Katherine, settling her wig.

'As ready as I'll ever be,' I said. 'Albert's wired to say he'll be at the Jollity.'

'Wonderful. Are my teeth all right?' She bared them at me.

'Beautiful, like polished jet. Now stop admiring yourself and come along.'

'Good luck, ladies,' said Selina, turning from the mirror where Ellen was helping her put her make-up on. She still looked pale, but a little happier. Perhaps the doctor was right, and getting back to the stage would help her.

'Thanks, Selina.' I squeezed her hand. 'Good luck to you too.'

'I'll need it.' She gave me a feeble squeeze back. 'If them stagehands drop my chair when they carry me off, I'll probably break in pieces.'

'Break a leg, then,' said Katherine, and grinned at her.

'Ugh,' said Selina, and giggled. 'I heard your friend's act was almost as good as mine. I'd like to meet her sometime. Maybe I could teach her a trick or two.' She winked.

'We'll introduce you soon and you can trade ideas,' said Connie. 'Tina's been busy with her other job, not to mention a bit of research for us. But I can imagine the two of you as a double-act — you'd be hilarious.'

Reg was waiting outside the changing room for us. 'I thought you were never coming,' he said. 'Ron's been hopping like a ginger bunny for the last ten minutes.'

'Perfection takes time,' said Katherine, patting her frizzy wig. 'Anything new from Bermondsey, Reg?'

Reg sucked his teeth. 'I'm narrowing it down, Miss C. It's a funny area, all alleys and passages, like a rabbit warren. Maybe I should send Ron down.'

'At last,' said Ron, when we joined him in the foyer. 'Thought you'd got lost on your way out. Cab's waiting.'

He opened the door for us, and Sam Webster, sitting on the box, raised his hat. 'Evening ladies, where to?'

I stood on tiptoe, and whispered in his ear. 'Awright. In you get.'

Katherine did as she was told, I followed, and Reg and Ron brought up the rear. Eventually we were all settled, and Ron tapped the glass. 'Off we go cabbie, it's showtime!'

CHAPTER 18
Katherine

*'I bought some lovely sweeties,
They're tasty as can be,
My friends all eat 'em, yes they do,
It isn't only me.'*

Three nights, five music halls each night. By Wednesday evening, I was beginning to worry I'd dance in my sleep. If I'd ached from a few hours in a factory, now my feet were sore and my toes bled. I came home every night to a foot-bath filled with Epsom salts. My mouth was dry from the court plaster, my skin breaking out from the make-up and my hair dull from being crammed under a wig. It had to be worth it. When it was all over, and Mr Templeton had paid our wages, I would give the whole of my portion to a society for retired dancers, if I had to start one myself.

Connie was spending half her life gargling honeyed water. She was making up for missing bedtime by spending extra time in the nursery and Bee had begun mimicking the whispering rasp she'd adopted to protect her voice. I'd half-jokingly suggested to Mr Templeton that he ought to record Connie on a phonograph and play that at full volume to give her a rest, but he growled 'Phonograph will kill the music-hall star,' and stormed off.

James and Albert entrusted our safety between venues to Ron, who escorted us from music hall to music hall, while they mingled backstage and in the various audiences to sense any reaction to our song. Not that this was hard to gauge — by that third evening, the auditorium was singing louder than we were, which at least gave Connie some respite. They also kept a lookout for Mr Sweet, but he seemed to have lost interest in us completely. Perhaps the lack of overt reference to Crystal Kisses had satisfied him.

In the penultimate venue, the Odyssey, I skipped on stage in my multicoloured checked dress, pulled a moue and with my hand to my brow scanned the audience.

'Where's my best boy?' I called. 'He said he had something to give me!'

'I bet he did, darling!'

'But he's got what I want!' I put out my bottom lip.

'I know what you want, ducks!' yelled a woman.

'Yeah!' said someone else. 'Crystal Kisses! "My boy is sweeter than —"'

'I don't know *what* you mean!' I shouted, as loud as I could, and signalled to the band to play our introduction. The heckler was drowned out as the audience joined in with our own song. After the third encore I drew our performance to an end, skipped off stage and with a last kiss blown to the audience, collapsed against Connie.

'And we still have the finale at the Merrymakers,' she groaned.

'I'm not sure I can keep this up,' I said, lifting one throbbing foot off the floor for a moment before limping down the steps towards the stage door and Sam's waiting cab. 'I was putting weight on but now I'm losing it again. I'm sure I'm wearing my legs down, too. Do I appear shorter than usual?'

'No, but that's because your wig is expanding on its own. Come on Katherine, we're all behind, much like your dress.'

The narrow alley beside the theatre was dark and the cobbles slippery. The drizzle which had been non-stop for days had become heavier. Connie and I, wrapped in our cloaks, huddled together with Ron under his enormous umbrella. The thought entered my exhausted head as we emerged onto the slick pavement that we must look like the most ridiculous mushroom, and I started to giggle. My feet slipped and I toppled us a little sideways.

'Whatever's the matter with you?' admonished Connie.

Ron helped us into the carriage and I explained.

'Only you would think of that,' she said. 'I hope you didn't twist your ankle though.'

'No, but I wish I'd had time to change my shoes,' I mourned. My dancing slippers were still drenched when we returned to the Merrymakers. Our final routine was a little longer, with a bit of repartee between me and an up-

and-coming comedian called Eric. Just as Felicity Velour was *almost* a lady, Eric was *almost* a millionaire.

'How's the latest scheme, Eric?' I asked, looking coy. 'Will you be able to escort me to the South of France like you promised?'

''e'll go dahn sarf somewhere if you let 'im!' heckled someone in the audience.

'I say!' declaimed Eric as I hid my face behind a fan. 'Miss Velour is a lady. A real proper miss. Have respect. Well, Felicity, it's like this. I've withdrawn some of my savings —'

He made a show as if to withdraw a pocket watch, realised it wasn't there and simultaneously, from above the stage, a huge pawnbroker's sign dropped down over his head. The audience guffawed.

'— and I'm after a business to invest in. Have you heard of anything? I want something which could make me a millionaire — that people can't get enough of? A sure thing.'

'I have,' I said, 'but there's a price to be paid.'

'Who cares?' argued Eric. 'As long as *I'm* not paying it — I mean to be rich!' He stepped a little to the side as I stood centre stage in my damp shoes and spread my arms.

'Well then...

> *I bought some lovely sweeties,*
> *They're tasty as can be,*
> *My friends all eat 'em, yes they do,*
> *It isn't only me.'*

How I got through the routine without breaking an ankle is anyone's guess. Fortunately, I realised that the audience put my slipping down to the act and therefore exaggerated it to make it look as if the effect of the mystery confectionery was making me stumble and reel. It wasn't so far from the truth of what had happened to Selina.

We did two encores before Mr Templeton took pity on us and brought down the curtain.

At the stage door, as ever, waited a crowd of fans — male and female — enduring the rain to speak to their favourite performer, or, in the case of some of the dancing girls, take them home. Even without my make-up and costume, I was jostled.

'You're her, ain't you?' hissed a man. 'F'licity?'

'She ain't no-one,' growled Ron, barging his way through. 'F'licity goes aht another way.'

'You sure? Which? I wanna see her.'

Then another voice in the darkness, a female voice, murmured close to my ear. 'You must be missing your little 'un…'

I couldn't tell if she was addressing me or Connie or one of the other performers emerging into the alley, but somehow it both chilled me and made my heart ache.

'Did you hear that?' I murmured to Connie as we finally climbed inside the homeward-bound cab.

'What?' she whispered, already trying to rest her voice. Even in the darkness, I could tell how tired she was as she settled against the seat.

'Nothing.'

***

We convened in the office the following morning at eleven. Reg had sent a telegram to say he would be a little late, but Tina was there, brewing coffee for us to drink with the sticky buns Connie had brought.

While we waited for Reg, I read out James's written report. He too had found the factory friendly while secretive. That was to be expected since competition was fierce. If either of us had been perceived to be spies for another company, it was no wonder we'd been dismissed.

Connie and I told Tina how the previous evening's tour had gone. 'Someone started singing the original Crystal Kisses song in the Odyssey,' said Connie. 'Neither of us are sure if it was coincidental or whether there was something behind it. Ron had no idea who the heckler was, but how could he? The auditorium was crowded.'

'Anything else?'

I thought of the voice in the darkness but shook my head. She could have been talking to anyone. I was not the only parent in the cast. The truth was that I felt sensitive about Ed. Not just missing him, but feeling guilty too. On the one hand I wished I were with him, and on the other, glad I was free to do as I pleased. Connie, I knew, was finding the whole thing a terrible struggle.

'Well,' said Tina, 'I'm sorry to say all that gossiping and I'm not so much further forward either.' She contemplated her tea as if scrying. 'I dropped all the hints I could. There's definitely something in the air about Crystal Kisses but it's hard to establish what. Some disapprove of sweets as indulgent and sinful, some see them as innocent and an alternative to sin, some have no views on the sinfulness but wonder about wasted money. Most think it's a kind of mania and are either happy to join in or rather suspicious. I dropped hints about the "club" which Tamar belonged to. No-one admitted anything, but I sensed more than one person knew what I meant. I pinned Caster and Fleet cards to noticeboards as you suggested, and hopefully someone will come forward.'

'I'm sorry it's been a waste of time,' I said.

'Oh, I wouldn't say that,' Tina grinned. 'Half the reason I joined all these groups anyway was to get ideas for Mrs Minchin, in case she ever found people weren't writing in with ludicrous enough problems to solve.' Her eyes widened with her grin. 'Mind you, some of the confidences I hear are too hair-raising to publish. That's regardless of class, education or religious views. Bizarrely, the mention of Crystal Kisses has opened a floodgate of confessions. I have material for months. Hark! Is that a soft foot I hear?'

A series of thumps indicated Reg's imminent arrival. He burst through the door like a hurricane, hung his dripping coat and hat on the rack, swept up the biggest bun from the plate and flung himself into a chair. 'Sorry I'm late, ladies, I bin following a lead,' he said, and took a huge bite of his bun. 'Mmm, cherries,' he mumbled.

Connie handed him a cup of coffee and we waited as he munched, willing him to eat quicker without choking.

'Well?' I said as he swallowed and took a gulp of coffee. 'Have you found the Bermondsey link?'

'Not exactly,' he confessed. 'Or rather, I feel like it's at my fingertips, just out of sight, like I'm always looking in the wrong direction. Like Alice through the thingummy.'

'Looking Glass?'

'That's the one. No, but this is the thing.' He took another mouthful of bun and we waited again. I resisted the urge to shake him. 'I was standing near some bill-stickers wondering which way to try next and one o' them said, "We need the latest Crystal Kisses one — when's it due?" And the other one said. "It'll be in Greenland by now. We should get it by noon."'

'Greenland?' said Connie. 'How could it be in Greenland and get here for noon? And if that's where the printers is, what are we going to do?' But I noticed Tina had sat forward.

'That's what I thought for a minute,' said Reg. 'Then I realised.'

'Greenland Dock,' said Tina. 'They're being brought into Greenland Dock. They're printed abroad.'

'That's hopeless,' I said. 'How can we find out where?'

'You need the right man in your bed,' said Tina.

Connie nearly spat out her coffee. 'I don't think —'

Tina grinned. 'I didn't mean you, I meant me. And I do mean my husband. Mr Hamilton gets his goods through Greenland Dock. Let's see what we can find out.'

CHAPTER 19
Connie

'This feels nice,' I said, leaning against Albert as Tredwell drove through the streets at a leisurely pace.

Albert squeezed me a little tighter. 'What, being with me?'

'Partly.' He raised his eyebrows in mock-surprise. 'I mean, doing something out in the open for a change.'

My telephone call to Albert on Monday had borne fruit. As it turned out, Mr Fraser was a member of the Carlton Club, an institution to which Albert had a standing invitation via Moss, who was a member when in town. A telephone call to Moss had secured a favour, and that evening, after our stint in every music hall in town (or so it seemed), Albert reported that we were invited for a tour of the factory on Friday. 'Oh, and the model housing,' he said casually. 'I told him that we were clandestine philanthropists.'

'Are we?'

'I donate money quietly to various charities. That will do if he asks questions.'

'What did you think of him, Albert?'

Albert frowned. 'You probably won't like this, Connie, but he seemed genuine. Honest, to the point of being blunt.'

I sighed. 'That's the impression I got, too.' Could Katherine and I have been pursuing something that wasn't there? But then I thought of Tamar shivering in bed, and Selina, thin and pale, and little Agnes scrabbling in the gutter. There had to be some truth in it.

Mr Fraser was waiting for us at the factory gates, even though we were a few minutes early. 'There you are!' he said, beaming. 'Through the gate, and then you can tie up the horse at the lodge. Our gateman will watch him while your driver has refreshment.'

'That's very kind,' I said. 'I believe we met at the Lansdowne Gallery?'

Mr Fraser's eyes widened, as did his grin. 'Why, so we did! Mrs Lamont, I presume?'

'That's right,' I said, smiling, and he kissed my hand with old-fashioned gallantry.

Once disembarked, we were taken into the factory itself, Mr Fraser talking all the way. 'It's wonderful to see our workers pulling the sugar, it really is, but I must ask you to stay well back. The sugar has to be extremely hot to allow them to work it, and I wouldn't want you to get burnt. Our workers all have extensive safety training before they commence in the sugar room.'

He was right. It was wonderful to see the men deftly stretching the sugar, which came in a variety of lurid colours, then cutting it into tiny pieces which others took and rolled until they were perfect spheres.

'What sweets will these become?' I asked.

'These are one of our best lines,' said Mr Fraser. 'Have you heard of Crystal Kisses?'

I tried to keep my face as composed as possible. 'I have, yes. I must confess they are a little too sweet for me.'

His face fell a fraction. 'That's a shame. Although they are aimed at children. We put fruit flavourings into them to get them to try the real thing in summer. So many children refuse to eat anything unfamiliar, and it's a terrible shame to waste Nature's bounty. Look!' He pointed at several different-coloured sweets forming into spheres. 'That's a raspberry, and a blackcurrant, and that one's a lime.'

'What a good idea,' said Albert, and I honestly couldn't tell if he were serious or not.

'Have you done any research into whether children eat more fruit after they've eaten the sweets?' I asked.

'Regrettably, not yet,' said Mr Fraser. 'It's a new line, you see, and I must admit that we were caught napping. We didn't expect them to do half as well as they have. It was a suggestion from our new production manager. I'd introduce you, but I don't think he's here.' He craned his neck this way and that, as if the missing man might be visible from a slightly higher perspective.

'So is that why you bought the painting?' I asked.

'Exactly so!' Mr Fraser beamed. 'I mean, who could resist those little faces? That picture of innocence? And fruit-flavoured sweets will do people a sight more good than hard liquor and late nights. They're practically a tonic!'

'Your production manager must be a very clever man,' Albert observed.

'Oh, he is, he is. I wasn't sure about him at first, I confess, but he has proved his worth a thousand times. Old lines have been cleared, failing products discontinued... He's a breath of fresh air. Good heavens, here he is! Your ears must be burning, young man!'

A slight, sandy-haired figure was hurrying towards us. 'Mr Fraser —'

'Mr Sweet! I was just talking about you!'

If ever I deserved applause, that was the moment. My countenance wanted to rearrange itself into goggle-eyed shock, but I kept it firmly under control. I know I did; for if my expression had reflected my inner emotions, Albert would surely have dug me in the ribs. 'Only good things, Mr Sweet,' I said, offering my hand.

'That is pleasing to hear,' he replied, taking my hand and executing a jerky little bob, for all the world like a wind-up toy. While Mr Fraser had addressed him as 'young man', Mr Sweet looked about forty-five, with a reddish beard, pale-blue eyes, and a complexion tending to pink. He also had a slight stoop, as if he had perhaps spent a little too much time bending over hot sugar. 'Mr Fraser, might I have a word?'

'Of course!' Mr Fraser took him by the arm, much as he had carried off Mr Landy a few days before, and they withdrew about ten yards' distance.

'What do you think?' I murmured to Albert, as we gazed at the men on a different station, who appeared to be making humbugs.

'Apart from feeling hungry —'

'Oh, honestly —'

'He isn't behaving like a man with anything to hide.'

Mr Sweet — *the* Mr Sweet, for there couldn't be more than one — was talking rapidly, his head close to Mr Fraser's, and looking in our direction. Mr Fraser threw his head back and laughed, and then ambled towards us. 'Mr Sweet is protective of his namesakes,' he chuckled. 'I assured him that you are not in the trade, nor planning to pass on our trade secrets, but he wouldn't have it. We are banished to the packing room.'

We watched women in hairnets pack chocolates and sweets into boxes, moving swiftly and efficiently, like automata. I couldn't imagine Katherine working there at all. 'How long did you say Mr Sweet had been with you?' I asked.

'Six months,' said Mr Fraser, his eyes on the boxes as they piled up. 'We entered into a new business arrangement, and took on additional staff as we expanded.'

'Oh, I see.'

'He knows the trade inside out — bred to it, like myself, and has worked in every branch. He'll be a wonderful help to my nephew when I retire.'

'I'm sure that won't be for a long time yet,' said Albert, with forced jollity.

'I'm seventy, you know,' said Mr Fraser, with an air of quiet pride. 'The new generation must take over at some point. Anyway, let's go and see the office.'

We didn't see much of it, for a tall, grey, clerkly figure strode up before we were fairly into the room. 'I'm so sorry,' he said, glancing at Albert and me, 'but our clerks are reaching the balance for the month, and they are at a delicate stage.' Certainly men in striped trousers were carrying ledgers this way and that across the room, looking sidelong at us. Everyone was very contained, very composed, and again the thought of James in that room was beyond my imagination.

Mr Fraser huffed. 'Very well, Mr Pearson. Since I am not welcome in my own factory, I shall take our visitors to see the housing. Unless you have any objections to that?'

Mr Pearson inclined his head politely. 'Oh no, not at all, Mr Fraser. Normally we would be more than glad to receive visitors, but we must put our business requirements first.'

'I suppose,' grumbled Mr Fraser. 'You go and balance the books, then. On your head, if you must.' He stalked out of the room, leaving us to follow.

His mood improved with the closing of the door. 'I'll take you to the nearest set of houses,' he said. 'My dream is to build a model village, but in London I have to make do with purchasing the best I can.' He led us to a back door, which gave onto a wrought-iron gate, and behind it was a row of neat little terraces, each with a pocket-sized front garden. He knocked at doors, and we met young mothers in spotless aprons, most with a baby or toddler on their hip, who all seemed pleased to see Mr Fraser, and grateful for the opportunity they had been given. Their parlours were clean, their grates well-blacked, their children healthy.

In one house the grandmother was at home, rocking a cradle with her foot while showing a toddler a picture book. 'John's taffy-pulling and Mrs John is packing,' she said, shushing the toddler. 'They have the baby in with them at night, and I sleep with little Charlotte and mind the children in the day. It's a godsend, I don't mind telling you. We was in rooms before, and they was dearer than this for a damp basement. That's London for you, though.'

Mr Fraser puffed up like a robin. 'I look after my workers,' he said. 'Not like some firms.'

'He does,' confirmed the woman. 'When William — my other son — was took bad, and he was in and out of the infirmary, Fraser's kept him on half pay and never denied him a thing. They even paid for the burial, and what other employer would do that?'

'We should probably be getting on,' said Mr Fraser, pulling a large silver watch from his waistcoat pocket.

'Did he pull taffy, too?' asked Albert.

'He did,' said the woman, smiling as she jiggled the toddler on her knee. 'He was never as strong as John, though, so he went to train the other workers. I think it was just too much for him.'

'Thank you so much for your time,' said Mr Fraser. 'I have a meeting in ten minutes, and I would like to see our visitors off beforehand.'

As the front gate closed behind us Mr Fraser was all smiles and effusiveness. He hoped we had enjoyed our visit, and learnt about the factory, and looked forward to seeing Albert at the Carlton again soon. But I must admit I was relieved when we were in our carriage and heading towards Marylebone.

'They definitely have something to hide,' I proclaimed, leaning back in my seat and disarranging my hat in the process. 'Even though Mr Fraser seems completely innocent.'

'I sincerely hope that they don't,' Albert replied.

The tone of his voice made me sit up. 'Why? Isn't that what we've been trying to prove all along?'

'It isn't that.' He took my hand. 'You know Mr Sweet's name, but Mr Sweet knows *you*. When we left the factory floor, I saw him watching you. He's seen you before, for sure. And I have a feeling it might have been at the music hall.'

CHAPTER 20
Katherine

I was never sure afterwards whether I shook from fear or pride whenever I recalled the shouting match with Mr Templeton.

'What about my audience?' he bellowed. 'You promised!'

'Bother your audience!' I bellowed back. 'It isn't safe for us to do the last two performances.'

'And there's me thinking you were a lady that'd keep her word! You bin mixing with the rough sort too long!'

'You saying we're common?' shouted Selina from the wings.

'You know you are!' bawled Mr Templeton.

'No she's not!' I shrieked. 'And nor am I! But Connie and I aren't doing it any more!'

'What 'appened to women speaking soft, gentle and low?'

'I don't know and I don't care! You've got a chorus full of potential — use one of them!'

Mr Templeton suddenly calmed down and lit his cigar. 'Cor, you're wasted in the music hall, Miss Caster,' he said with a grin. 'You're a proper harridan when you're roused. You ought to be doing Shakespeare. Though I'm not sure you're cut out for any simpering parts. The Lady in the Scottish Play now — I can see you inciting murder. I'm dead impressed.'

With some effort I calmed my breathing and tried to formulate an apology, but Mr Templeton waved it away.

'Nah — you're right. Audiences are fickle things,' he said. 'Leave them wanting more and come back with something new soon.'

'Don't worry,' I reassured Connie as we left. 'We've probably done all we can through the halls anyway. Everything will be fine.'

I squeezed her hand. It's small wonder she squeaked. I was trying to squash my sense of disquiet at the same time. Not to mention wondering if Mr Templeton had meant he could see me playing Lady MacBeth or one of the witches.

***

We met in the office at eight the following morning. An early start meant Connie had plenty of time to spend with her children afterwards and James and I could catch the lunch-time train to Berkshire to stay and then bring Ed home on Monday.

Now she and I sat typing up our notes while waiting for Mr Maynard's response to our report. I was sure that, despite the loose ends, our conclusion would convince him.

We need more time. People are becoming seriously ill and if there is no connection between Crystal Kisses and the samples, then whoever is sending the samples must be found and prosecuted.

'When his letter comes,' I said, 'let's treat ourselves in a coffee-shop while we read it. Tina won't be in today and Reg won't be either. He's out investigating —'

The door swung open and slammed against the wall. Reg stood before us, his face aglow, waving copies of the *Illustrated News* and the *Chronicle*.

'Good morning,' I said. 'We weren't expecting to see you. What have you found out?'

'Cor blimey,' he said. 'You don't know, do you?' He handed over the papers and turned to the second page of the illustrated one.

It was a sketch — pretty much a caricature — but it was Connie and me all right, her tall and striding, me scurrying in her wake like a pet. She was somehow both regal and bawdy, like a swaggering Britannia. I, grotesquely made-up, hair in an overblown style that dwarfed my head and skirts barely below my knees, looked like a wanton pixie. I thought of all the times I'd giggled at that sort of picture and felt ashamed.

Most ladies turn to charitable works rather than feel idle, but not Mrs Albert Lamont and Mrs James King. They turn to painting themselves and cavorting on the stage. Aha, you may think, The Bard or something modern — or maybe — given how they appear — 'School for Scandal'? Not so. Mrs Lamont and Mrs King have abandoned home and hearth for the low music hall, and not just one, but five! What an example they are setting their children! Let's hope that Mrs Lamont's daughters don't follow her lead.

Are their husbands men? If so — take control, Mr Lamont and Mr King! This is not the womanhood the Empire is built upon. For shame ladies — if you are ladies. For shame.

We stared aghast and then Reg pointed to *The Chronicle*. Its article was different in tone but the implication was identical.

Mrs Albert Lamont and Mrs James King, founders of the Caster and Fleet Agency, seem to have too much time on their hands. Not content with play-acting as amateur detectives, they have taken to the music hall with facetious songs apparently written to discredit a highly respected institution with innuendo and salacious scandal-mongering. Is this because one of them was fired from a position she had gained falsely in order to spy? Or because the other is bored with respectable Society? Who, should we ask, is behind their latest assignment? A rival company with scurrilous intent? Or is a certain government department poking where it's not wanted? Do the ladies think their agency is so important they will take up any job, no matter how dubious? Or is it simply that, as the modern kind of woman we are supposed to applaud, they would rather cavort on stage and drive around

London late at night, in the company of strange men, than look after their own homes?

Connie put her face in her hands.

Reg stood twisting his hands for a moment before, out of sheer need to do something, going to make tea.

I stared at those awful words, and then closed my eyes.

'Mrs King!' A familiar voice made me jump. Mr Maynard stood quivering in the doorway, two other newspapers in his hands.

One held a full-page advertisement.

Accept no substitutes!
Fraser's Sweets are pure enough for a babe in arms.
Health-giving fruit-filled Crystal Kisses provide a taste of summer all year round.
Don't let political interference ruin family businesses.
Fraser's — the only choice for decent families, decent mothers, decent homes.

The other held an article similar to the *Chronicle's* but in this case more forthright. Personal ownership of senior civil servants' shares in confectionery firms was publicised; and the senior civil servants named included Mr Maynard.

'What did you think you were doing?' he growled, slamming his fist on the desk. 'How dare you bring the Department into disrepute!' He paused, looked behind him and shut the door. His controlled voice was somehow more menacing than a bellow. 'Your investigation has made things ten times worse.' Straightening, he added more loudly as the door burst open again. 'I am ashamed you have any connection with me. In fact —'

'In fact...' said another voice. Chief Inspector Barnes stalked in, doffing his hat with a scowl dark enough to curdle the milk in Reg's hand. 'In fact, you are close to prosecution.'

He ushered forward a man I knew to be Mr Fraser but could barely recognise. Instead of the kindly old man in pictures, here was someone so angry I feared he would drop dead and his mouth worked as if he was chewing through a series of bad words to find the best one to spit out first. 'Defamation at the very least!' Spittle formed on his mouth even as his lip curled. He turned to Connie. 'I am disgusted to think I kissed your hand, Mrs Lamont. How could such a demure and obedient demeanour hide so sinful a heart? Fool am I for trusting the outward appearance!'

'But —' started Connie, her eyes full of tears.

'And as for you, Mrs King, I gather you pretended to be in need of work just to look round our factory. You, if anything, are worse than your colleague — painting yourself every evening, displaying flesh!'

'It wasn't like that!' I argued, feeling my heart thud, wanting to appeal to Mr Maynard but not daring to draw attention to him. 'You must have seen for yourself that my dress was decent and my make-up silly. I —'

'No!' Mr Fraser held up his hand. 'I have *not* seen for myself. I would not stoop so low as to enter such an establishment. But I have *heard* enough. I have had your song repeated to me. Defamation, plagiarism, espionage. Spies, both of you. Who paid you? This gentleman? No — clearly he is as revolted as I! A man you have cheated, no doubt. I shall make sure both of you are shown up as charlatans, money-grabbers, and immodest termagants with whom no decent person should associate. I shall — I shall —'

Chief Inspector Barnes put his hand out to restrain Mr Fraser. 'No threats, sir. But let me *warn* you, ladies,' he said, his face unreadable beyond its coolness. 'Desist any activity which will bring a prosecution. You need to restore your reputations. Both professional...' He looked us both up and down and then perused the caricature, 'and personal. Good day.' Donning his cap, he steered the still-spluttering Mr Fraser away.

Mr Maynard waited until they had departed, growled 'I'll pass this on to someone who can do a simple job properly,' and slammed his way out of the office.

Connie began crying in earnest. I put my arms round her and held her close. She was mumbling a series of names and I couldn't work out which was causing her the most misery: 'Albert, Bee, Mother, Father, the servants — oh what will they think?'

I didn't know what to do or say. I had my own list of names in my head. James could rise above it, but everyone else? The thought of my innocent little boy made my eyes fill with tears. It was nearly a week since I'd seen him. Would he recognise me or be too upset to come to me? And I'd brought shame on him.

I'd had enough. Connie and I had both had enough. Let

Mr Templeton fill his own stage. Let Mr Maynard find someone else to solve his wretched mystery.

***

When I finally returned home an hour later Tamar opened the door, and the smirk on her face told me she knew what had been in the press.

'Be sure to shake my coat out properly this time,' I said to her, holding my head high. 'Is the master here?'

'Yes ma'am. In his study, reading the papers.' She turned a snigger into a cough.

'I daresay you've been reading them too,' I said, resisting the urge to slam my hat onto the hall table and the hatpins into her. 'Well, you can decide for yourself what to believe, Tamar, but I expect the same service from you, and if you are not prepared to give it, you may go.'

'Oh no, ma'am.' Tamar looked stricken. 'This is a good place. I never believe what they say in the papers. It can't have been you what was in the music hall. You're far too fancy.'

'It *was* me,' I said. 'And you can make of that what you wish. I shall speak to the master. We are not to be disturbed.'

Inside the study, my composure collapsed. I flew into James's arms. 'Have you seen —?'

'I have,' he said. 'We've had worse things said in the press about you and me. We'll get through this.'

'I know, but this time it's Connie too.'

'She'll survive. No-one who knows either of you will believe anything bad. Anyone who does clearly isn't worth knowing.'

'That's not how Society works. And Connie goes about in it such a great deal.'

James said something very rude about Society. He kissed the top of my head and pulled me onto his lap.

My face was still burning with shame. 'I've had enough, James,' I said.

'Of the Merrymakers?'

'No. Of investigations. I want to — what did it say? *Return to hearth and home.* Build our family.' I felt James tense. 'I thought you *wanted* me to give up.'

'I'd like you in a different role,' he said. 'Absentee overseer, perhaps. Let Reg see what he can make of the business.'

'I'd like another baby, James.' This time I couldn't mistake his tension.

'We can't,' he said.

'Maybe we can. I know we never thought we'd have Ed, and maybe we'll never have another, but maybe we shall.'

'It's not like that —' James fidgeted and I moved away from him so I could look into his eyes. He swallowed, then reached to hold my face in his hands. 'The doctor told me Ed must be the last. There was . . . damage done, and you lost a lot of blood. You nearly died. I — I didn't know how to tell you. Neither of us did.'

'*Neither* of us? Who else knew? Does everyone but me know?'

'Not everyone,' said James. 'Just me, and Ada. I'm sorry, Katherine. I wanted to tell Connie but I didn't know how. I'd like another child too, but we can't. There's just the three of us, and you mean everything to me. Now do you understand why I want you to stop investigating? I can't risk losing you. I can't. I love you too much.'

CHAPTER 21
Connie

The office telephone shocked me out of a depressing reverie in which Albert and I — not to mention Katherine and James — were barred from every restaurant and place of note in London. I stared at it, willing it to stop ringing, but it shrilled on. Eventually, sick of the noise it made, I got up and lifted the receiver, bracing myself for a tirade. 'Good morning, Caster and Fleet Agency,' I said, and my voice was as flat and dull as I felt.

'I'm not sure I'd call it a *good* morning,' said Mother, crisply. 'What on earth is this rubbish I've just seen in the papers?'

My heart plummeted into my boots. 'I — I —'

'Can you explain yourself, Constance?'

My brain whirled. Katherine and I had travelled the music halls, gone undercover, inveigled our way into Fraser's factory... But we had done it all for a good reason.

'Yes,' I said. 'Yes, I can.'

'Then I shall be intrigued to hear it. Remind me where your — *office* — is again.'

I gave the address, barely able to believe I wasn't being shouted at.

'I shall be there as soon as possible. Some tea when I arrive would be nice. It has been rather a trying morning.' And Mother rang off.

***

It was as well that the office was already tidy; I lacked the energy to do more than sit and be miserable. What if my explanation did not satisfy Mother, and she disowned me, refused to see me, cut me in the street? I was working myself up to another burst of tears when a sharp rap at the door jolted me out of it. 'Come in,' I called, automatically, and Mother, immaculate as ever, swept into the room and bore down on me.

'Oh dear, Connie,' she said, and kissed me on the cheek.

The unexpected kindness was far worse than if she had shouted at me. 'I'm so sorry, Mother,' I sobbed.

'Nonsense. Do you have something to be sorry about?'

'Being made to look a fool,' I sniffled.

'And were you a fool?' Mother lifted my chin, and her steel-grey eyes looked into mine.

'What I was doing was part of our investigation,' I murmured. 'So no, I wasn't. Neither was Katherine, however silly her costume. I wasn't even on the stage.'

Mother frowned. 'So what were you doing?'

'I — was singing. For Katherine.'

Her mouth twitched. 'And you too nervous to sing in our drawing room.'

'I know,' I whispered.

'You've come a long way, Connie.' Her lip curled. 'So all this — to-do — is about one silly song in a music hall. Have people nothing better to talk about?'

'Apparently not,' I said, and out came the whole story, beginning with Mr Maynard's secret visit, up to the events at Fraser's factory. Mother sat taking it all in, like a dove-grey sphinx.

'It doesn't matter anyway,' I said. 'We won't be doing it any more.'

Mother's lips twitched a second time. 'I wouldn't be too sure of that, Connie.'

I gawped at her. 'What on earth do you mean, Mother?' I exclaimed.

'That's a bit more like it,' she said, putting her hands in her lap. 'Our telephone hasn't stopped ringing since eight o'clock this morning.'

'Oh no…' I wailed.

'Oh yes.' Mother had a distinct glint in her eye. 'People I haven't spoken to in five years have been telephoning to ask whether you really are a music-hall star, and which hall you perform at, and whether it is still possible to buy tickets. Lady Frobisher wants to bring a charabanc-full to see you. Some of them even asked about your agency. Oh, and a rather uncouth man called Templeton wanted to know where you were.'

A light tap at the door. 'Come in,' I called. It could be Mr Fraser, come back to threaten me again, or Chief

Inspector Barnes with his closed face. So long as Mother was on my side, I could bear it.

Albert peeped round the door. 'Good heavens — I mean, how nice to see you, Mrs Swift,' he said, advancing and taking her still-gloved hand. 'Sorry to burst in, Connie, but I had a feeling that if I rang first you'd probably tell me not to come.'

'You — don't mind?' I gazed up at my husband.

'He's got more sense than that,' said Mother, and we both looked round in surprise. 'I always thought marrying him was one of the best decisions you ever made, Connie.'

I goggled at her. 'Really?'

'Oh yes,' she said, rising to her feet. 'I may not have said so at the time, admittedly...' She allowed herself a small smile. 'You're a sensible woman, and usually right. I'll see myself out. Oh, and come to tea if you're free on Sunday. I don't know what hours you music-hall people keep.'

Albert and I waited until her footsteps had receded. '*A sensible woman, and usually right,*' I murmured. 'I might work that as a sampler.'

'You won't have time,' said Albert. 'Johnson has a list of calls for you to return, and a heap of telegrams for you to open.'

'For me?'

He nodded, and put his arms round me. 'I don't think it's quite the reaction that whoever wrote that article was aiming for,' he murmured into my ear.

'No...' I twisted my head round to kiss him. Then I froze. 'I *can't*,' I muttered. 'Mr Fraser came here and threatened us both, and Chief Inspector Barnes told us to close. He *warned* us.'

'Chief Inspector Barnes did?' Albert looked taken aback.

'Yes.'

'The same Chief Inspector Barnes who is sitting in our parlour?'

I blinked. 'Does he seem angry? He was earlier.'

Albert shook his head. 'He said he wanted to clear up a few things.'

'I feel like a character in a Shakespeare comedy,' I said dreamily. 'Things keep turning on their heads. The next thing I know, Mr Fraser will come in and offer to take me to the theatre.'

Albert snorted. 'You might have to wait a bit for that. As might I before I set foot in the Carlton again.'

***

'I had my hand forced, you see,' said the Chief Inspector, over a good lunch. 'My boss is a Quaker and a friend of Fraser's, so he told me to put the frighteners on you. Not in so many words, you understand, but his intention was clear.' He put his knife and fork together and sighed. 'Now I hoped you would take my meaning earlier, but coming as I did in the middle of the two shouting gentlemen, I'm not sure you did.'

'Neither am I,' I replied, pushing aside the rest of my potatoes and laying down my cutlery. 'What did you mean?'

'Well, sadly I haven't heard your song, and while I suspect Fraser hasn't a leg to stand on, since he's repeating hearsay, I advise you to check through it very carefully.'

'We're not stupid!' I cried.

'I thought not,' replied the Chief Inspector. 'I also told you to lie low until this has blown over. No overt activity, no new clients, no business in the agency's name.' He dropped one eyelid in a slow wink. 'However, what you do in your personal time, provided it is legal, is your own affair.'

Johnson put his head round the door. 'I've tried the number again, ma'am, and according to the servant Mrs King is still not at home.'

I sighed. 'If only I could tell Katherine all this.'

'I daresay you'll catch up with each other soon enough,' said Chief Inspector Barnes. 'Now, tell me exactly what you saw at Fraser's factory, and why you were there in the first place.'

***

'She *really* isn't at home, Mrs Bertie,' said Ada, leaning wearily on the doorframe. 'You can come in and have a look under the sofa if you want, but she's not there.'

'Have she and James gone to Hazelgrove?'

'No,' said James, entering the hall. 'We were meant to be getting the one o'clock train. And no, I don't know where she's gone.' He pushed his hair out of his eyes, and I saw the grief in his face.

'It'll all blow over, James, it's a nine days' wonder —'

'It isn't that,' he said, softly. 'It's something else. She said she wanted to be alone for a while.'

'Something else?' But I could see from James's face that it was between them.

'She probably won't want to see me, then,' I said.

James grimaced. 'She might. More than she wants to see me, anyway. Good luck, Connie.' He turned away abruptly and walked into the study, closing the door behind him.

'I can't report her missing,' said Ada. 'Mrs Kitty wouldn't thank me, and it's been enough of a day as it is. Messages and phone calls and I don't know what all. I expect you've had the same.'

I nodded, and suddenly Ada, wiry, bristling Ada, reached out and took my arm. 'She needs a good friend today.' She squeezed, briefly, then let go and closed the door.

***

Katherine wasn't at the tube station.

She wasn't at the Embankment.

She wasn't at our office.

She wasn't in the park where we had taken breaks, in the days when we had been valued employees of the Department.

I racked my brains for more ideas. *Some detective you are*, said the imp on my shoulder. *You can't even find your best friend.*

If she wanted to be alone, she wouldn't be with any of her friends. She'd be somewhere I wouldn't think to look, somewhere James wouldn't know, somewhere she went before she met me.

See? It's impossible, said the imp.

Before she met me... And I remembered a little figure curled into herself, reading a letter and toying with a plate of dismal stew, who had scowled at me when I spoke to her, the first time that we met.

I hurried down the street. Was the restaurant still there, even?

The lunch rush, if it could be called that, was long over, and it was almost empty save for a few late diners. I strained my eyes in the gloom, scanning the tables.

'Would you like a table, ma'am?' asked the waitress, hurrying forward with a menu.

In the corner a white face glanced up and, as quickly, down again.

'I'm not sure,' I said, advancing. 'I need to speak to my friend.'

Katherine was swaddled in a cloak, and her red hair was crammed into a shapeless hat. 'You found me,' she said, flatly.

'Yes. May I sit down?'

'It's a free country.' She sipped her cup of tea and broke a piece off a bun which was, from the look of it, being reduced to fragments.

'I called at your house. I have good news —'

'I'm glad someone has.' The bun lost another crumb.

'Do you want to tell me about it?'

Her green eyes showed none of their usual spark, and her shoulders stiffened. 'It isn't fair,' she said, to herself. 'Nothing's fair. Not ever. Not the case, and not this.'

And then she told me.

CHAPTER 22
Katherine

'He should have been honest,' I said, staring into my cup.

'He's so upset he's made you angry,' Connie answered.

I sighed. 'I'm not angry. I think I knew deep down. I'm just sad. He must be too. I shouldn't have walked out like that. But on top of everything else… I had to get away for a bit.' I raised my eyes. Across the table was the same dear friend who had been a stranger so few years ago. 'I'm glad you found me, but now you'll be afraid I'll be jealous of your children. And I shan't be. Even if you have a million.'

Connie reached for my hand and gave a small smile. 'I'm not sure my figure could stand a million. I might stop at a hundred.'

I attempted a grin. 'Good idea. I should remember how lucky I am to have Ed.'

Connie bit her lip. 'I know it's not exactly the same — but remember how you've always said the gap between you and Margaret was too big for you to play together, but at least you had Albert? Cousins aren't so bad. Ed can play with my children any time. He and George are thick as thieves already.'

'Thank you.' My anger had indeed receded, if it had ever been there, but the disappointment remained and the words tumbled out before I could stop them. 'I'm not surprised at Ada. She can keep more secrets than a pyramid. But James…'

'I suspect James didn't want to believe it himself,' said Connie. 'You were so pleased to have Ed, who's strong and healthy. Maybe James thought he need never say.'

I withdrew my hand and rubbed my eyes. 'Oh, what a terrible day,' I said. 'We've utterly failed. Our names are in the mud. I've got you in a mess again. And now I've to make peace with James, then face everyone at Hazelgrove. Whatever will they say about what's in the paper? I'll never be able to explain.'

'It's not as bad as you think,' said Connie. The triumphant note in her voice made me raise my head. 'Come on. Let's go somewhere with more, er, choice on the menu. I've got a lot to tell you.'

***

After sending a brief telegram to James saying I was safe and would be home by three, we found a quiet restaurant and settled down for lunch. I might have eaten more if I'd spent less time with my mouth open as she talked. As the cold, half-eaten first course was removed I realised how hungry I was, and to Connie's delighted surprise ordered a piece of Bakewell tart for dessert.

'So,' she said. 'What shall we do? Roll over and play dead? Keep quiet like we've been told?' Her words were passive but her eyes flashed.

I recalled the morning's shouting: the accusations and subtle threats. My face burned again as I thought of the words and pictures, libelling us both. And *we* were the ones being threatened with prosecution.

Suddenly I was no longer ashamed but angry. Mr Maynard's withdrawal of support to save his own hide, Chief Inspector Barnes's duplicity, Mr Fraser's assumptions based on gossip churned into an inner storm of rage.

'We shall not!' I proclaimed with such determination a frail old gentleman on the next table tipped his wineglass over and Connie leaned back as if someone had opened an oven door in her face. I lowered my voice. 'Or at least, *I* shan't. James and I can catch a later train. I won't drag you along if you don't want to.'

'Huh,' said Connie in her best music-hall accent. 'Try and stop me.'

I checked my watch and rose. It was two o'clock. 'I think we need an emergency office meeting.'

'You'll never get home for three.'

I hesitated for a second. I remembered my husband's face, and the pain in it. He should have been sharing, not hiding it, and we should have been comforting each other. When would we learn? 'We need James at the meeting. Albert, too. If Caster and Fleet are going under — they're going under very noisily.'

'Chief Inspector Barnes said to keep our heads down.'

'He can keep his own head down,' I retorted. 'I'm keeping mine up. Preferably with an even more ridiculous wig.'

***

We had not been able to get word to Reg. His mother Maria said he'd come home at ten, looking like thunder, to say he would be out all day till tea-time. We left a message to tell him to come to the Merrymakers as early as he could.

Now it was early evening and he still hadn't arrived, but a telegram had come to say he would be there by eight-thirty. Tina was on stage doing a double act with Selina, and by the sound of things it was bringing the house down. Mr Templeton had been into the dressing room twice to complain about the nobs clogging up the street with their nobby carriages and wretched charabanc. I had never seen anyone so happy while complaining. Albert had meanwhile got word backstage that Mr Sweet was near the front.

'Are you ready?' said Connie.

'Are you? You don't have to do this.'

She swallowed and leaned forward to examine herself in the glass. 'It's not *me*, is it?'

'No,' I said. 'That's how you do it. It's not you. It's someone else. At least you look almost nice.' I was in a white dress on which had been sewn large brightly-coloured circles. My head ached under an immense Marie-Antoinette style wig in purple, to which yellow tartan bows had been attached.

'Are you certain that's not Fraser tartan?' muttered

Connie for the fourteenth time.

'Positive,' I reassured her. 'It's McLeod. Much better effect.'

Tina and Selina burst into the dressing room as the dancers clattered out to provide a brief intermission between their act and ours.

'That was fun,' said Tina. 'The man you told us to look for seems relaxed, although not as much as he is when the dancers are on stage.' She dropped her voice to a whisper. 'Typical stage-door johnny? Or something else?'

'Miss C & Miss F!' Ron called. It was our turn to go on stage. Connie lurked as usual while I pranced on stage to join Mr Templeton.

'How do F'licity!' he boomed. 'Thought we'd seen the last of you.'

'You can't keep a good girl down,' I said, simpering and pulling an innocent pose. Loud guffaws burst from the audience and I wagged my finger at them. 'It's time to remind you I am a lady!'

The band struck up and I began a new version of the song I'd sung the first time I'd gone on stage at the Merrymakers.

I'm a lady you know,
A real proper miss.
How could I know
I'd get caught by a Kiss?
They thought I'd give up
And sing out no more,
But no-one tells lies

About F'licity Velour.
All that I want
Is for danger to pass,
But someone's trying to push me
Flat on my —

I turned to the wings. 'Miss Fleet, why are you hiding? Everyone, welcome my friend — another proper lady! Come on out, don't be shy.'

Connie emerged from the wings. She was dressed as Britannia in floating Grecian robes, and her hair was piled on her head under a coronet. The make-up on her face, which would simply make her features show across an auditorium, looked ridiculous up close. I hoped her mother and all her friends were far enough away not to be able to see. Whether they could or not, the cheers from the boxes were louder than ever.

'Well, I don't know,' squeaked Connie, and finding her nerve, managed a more carrying tone. 'Did you see what they put in the paper about Caster and Fleet? They don't know the half!'

'I know! We're *much* more interesting than that!'

Arm in arm we marched round the stage singing:

They say we're being naughty,
But we're proper ladies us,
We're more British than Buckingham Palace,
Or a London omnibus.
We've still got lots of energy,
Of that there is no doubt —

What you should know about us is
We like to find things out!

We both pulled enormous magnifying glasses from our bodices at this point and proceeded to spy through them at each other and the audience before continuing our song and dance.

I caught Connie's hands and we skipped off stage to wild applause and cheers. My wig was awry and one set of Connie's false eyelashes had fallen off. 'Never again,' she said. 'Never ever again.'

'Admit it, it was fun,' I answered. 'Anyway, that told them. They can't accuse us of doing anything but sending ourselves up.'

'While giving the message that we can't be put down.'

'Exactly.'

We made our way to the dressing room to find Reg, Tina and James outside. Reg was bouncing and bursting to speak.

'Not here,' whispered Tina. Then more loudly, 'I want some fresh air, don't you?'

It was raining in the alley beside the theatre, but at least it was empty. We huddled under two umbrellas while Reg delivered his news.

'I wasn't going to let them put me off. I knew there was something to find out and I'd had a brainwave — just never had time to tell you before you sent me home. So I followed it up. See — Caster & Fleet have a PO box address, don't they? But deliveries come to the ground floor of the address the office is in. They could be in a different building altogether.'

'That's true,' said Connie. 'Are you still following the postboys around?'

'I am, and one of them dropped his bag. A pile of identical cards fell out. The postboy was in a right two and eight. He scrabbled them all up out the puddles and headed off. Well, he'd only left one behind, hadn't he? So me, I'm a good citizen, I picked it up and couldn't fail to notice it was what we was after. Of course I was honour-bound to give it back. Eventually. Then I followed him.'

Reg stopped to take breath. 'So to cut a long story short, the PO box address is a shop. Not a factory. So I was feeling down, but then someone came out and he was muttering about everything in his bag being damp and I realised he had those cards and was going somewhere with them. So I followed *him*. It was like following a rat, he sort of scuttled. I thought he was gonna go down a sewer any minute, but he didn't. He took me straight to a factory — and from the smell, it makes sweets.'

'Reg — that's —' I didn't know how to finish. Dangerous? Brave? Wonderful? Reg was all three.

'So now we know where the PO box address is and exactly where the factory is. It ain't in Bermondsey, it's in Southwark.'

'That fits with what Mr Hamilton said,' muttered Tina. 'I asked him about Greenland Dock and he said it was practically all Baltic timber going through there. What would those ships be doing with sweetie posters? I thought those men had got it wrong, but now I see. The posters aren't picked up from Greenland Dock because they've come from abroad. It's because the dock's no distance from Southwark, and handy for this factory Reg has found. The whole thing's a gigantic red herring.'

'A red herring that we've smoked out,' I said grimly. 'But now what do we do?'

CHAPTER 23
Connie

So much for a day of rest, I thought, as I opened a bleary eye. Katherine and James would be safely at Hazelgrove, and hopefully still asleep after their journey the previous evening.

I, however, had work to do.

Following Reg's news Katherine had offered to stay, but I could see the reluctance in her face, even under the greasepaint.

'Go and rest for a day,' I had said. 'We can handle anything that happens.'

Katherine looked at me narrowly. 'You're plotting, aren't you?'

'Me?' I attempted an innocent expression. 'I have no idea what you mean.'

Her eyes narrowed further.

'And if you don't know what it is, you can't be blamed.'

Katherine grinned. 'That's better. But do be careful.'

***

Reg would be arriving at ten. Before that, though, I had another task — going through the telegrams and letters we had received. James had brought the ones sent to Katherine, and with those delivered to the office, I found myself gazing at a sizeable heap. Most of them were simple messages of support from friends, acquaintances, and even strangers; but some ran deeper.

Don't stop what you're doing, said one letter, written on cheap white notepaper. *I see those people handing out the sweets, and what the children are like afterwards. It oughtn't to be allowed.* It was signed '*A Well-Wisher*'.

I sighed, and put it into the growing 'anonymous' pile. If only we could tell people about all these letters…

Letters… I sprang up and went to the telephone.

'What time d'you call this?' asked Tina, when she finally came to the receiver.

'I'm sorry, Tina. I didn't wake you, did I?'

'Course not, I've been up since seven. I'm that far behind with Mrs Minchin that I'm up to my ears in post.'

'Oh good.'

'I'm glad you approve. Is this a social call?'

'I've had an idea.'

Silence. Then 'Go on.'

I explained.

'We've never done anything like that before,' said Tina.

Silence again.

'But there's no reason why we can't do it. I'll need help though, if I'm to get it done for Monday. That's the absolute deadline.'

'I'll work through the night for you if I have to,' I said. 'But I have something to do first.'

***

'Too short,' said Albert. 'I can see your ankles.'

'You don't usually complain,' I sniffed, going into the bedroom. 'If only you were six inches shorter and a bit wider.'

'But I'm not,' he said, smugly.

Reg had brought a selection of clothing and two friends, Dickie and Smudge, who were currently worrying Mrs Jones in the kitchen. Reg himself was hovering on the landing, outside the closed door of my boudoir. 'Any luck, Miss F?' he called.

'It's just finding trousers. Everything else is fine.'

'Oh.' A pause. 'You don't have to come, Miss F —'

'Yes I do,' I said. 'I'm not having you snooping around a potentially dangerous factory on your own.'

'But Mr F, I mean Mr L is coming —'

'Exactly. I have to look after him.' I buttoned up the final pair of trousers and adjusted the braces. There. With a loose jacket, I would pass at a distance. On a Sunday everything ought to be quiet anyway.

Albert's mouth twitched as I opened the door. 'You'll do,' he said, getting up and putting his arms round what was left of my waist. 'Do you know, I rather like you in trousers.'

'Don't get too used to it,' I said. 'Although they're a great deal easier to wear than those Grecian robes last night. I was convinced they were going to fall off.'

'Now that *would* have been a show,' he said, and kissed me.

'Mind my hat!' I grabbed the brim and held it on with both hands. 'If my hair comes loose, I'm done for.'

'Maybe later, then,' said Albert.

***

Tredwell dropped us off in a back street near Southwark Bridge. 'Is it far from here, Reg?' I asked.

'Few minutes' walk,' said Reg. 'I'm gonna take us round the long way, though. Give you time to get used to those boots.'

I nodded and stuck my hands in my trouser pockets, as I had been told. Dickie and Smudge had taken a sort of lead, sauntering along as if tomorrow would do, and I tried to imitate their slouching air of indolence. Even Reg seemed different; whether it was because he was with his friends, or trying to fit in with the area, I could not be sure. I had felt extremely self-conscious when, following instructions, I had added coal-dust grime to my neck and face. Now, though, I was grateful to hide behind it. We were in a mainly industrial area, among deserted workshops, and the only people we saw were children swinging and climbing on the silent machinery, who paid us no attention at all.

'Slow down,' muttered Reg, and Dickie and Smudge came casually to heel. 'It's in the next street,' he continued, in the same low tone. 'Big place. Shaw and Sons, it's called. I've only seen the front, cos I couldn't hang about, but there'll be a goods entrance. I suggest we split in two, walk round the back if we can, and check for open windows an' gaps — anywhere we might be able to get in. But don't try till we've all looked. And keep an eye out for watchmen.' He moved to my side. 'If I say run, Miss F, run, hard as you can.'

I gulped. We rounded the corner, and before us was a wide brown-brick building, perhaps two storeys tall. It had few windows, and those were set high in the walls; but what caught my attention was the plumes of smoke rising from the chimneys.

'They're working,' I breathed.

'On a Sunday,' said Albert. 'I bet Mr Fraser doesn't know that.'

'Damn.' Reg frowned for a moment. 'All right. Change of plan. You two,' — he looked at Albert and me — 'find the goods entrance and hang round for a bit. We're gonna march in the front door and see if they've got any work going. Don't worry, we ain't gonna take it, but if it gets us inside for a minute or two it's worth a go. We'll meet you round the back. If we're gone more than an hour, go home and call the police.'

'Right,' said Albert, sounding much more businesslike than I felt. 'Good luck, lads.' He strolled off, whistling, and I had no choice but to catch him up.

An odd smell hung in the air; sickly sweet, but with a metallic tang that caught the back of my throat. 'We won't stay too long,' murmured Albert. 'That stink's enough to make you ill, never mind eating whatever comes out.'

I forced myself to slow down, to look around me and not stare at the factory; but my gaze kept returning to it. What were they doing inside? I remembered the sugar-pullers and the packers at Fraser's — but there the air had been sweet with subtle smells of fruit and vanilla. The air here smacked you round the face with its harshness.

At last we were at the back of the factory, which was protected by a tall iron fence with a double gate. It was open, and a man was opening the great factory doors for a waiting wagon.

Albert lit a short clay pipe and leaned against a solitary tree, watching the proceedings. The gatekeeper, short and squat, saw him. 'Come an' give a hand, then!' he shouted, angrily.

'Wossit worth?' Albert shouted back.

'Penny to 'elp me unload this lot.' The man jerked a thumb at the driver, who was sitting on the box of the wagon as if he had nothing to do with any of it. 'E's about as much use as a chocolate teapot. Says after what happened to his mate 'e ain't touching it.'

'Awright.' Albert unpeeled himself from the tree.

'For God's sake put that pipe out! D'you want the whole place to go up?'

Albert handed the pipe to me and I put it in my mouth, trying not to breathe anything in. 'What you got on there?' he asked the driver.

'Never you mind,' was the phlegmatic reply. 'Just you do your job and sling yer 'ook.'

'Nice to meet you too,' said Albert, tipping his flat cap.

The gatekeeper put two planks in position, and they began to roll the barrels off the wagon. 'Easy does it,' said the gatekeeper. 'That's it. Thought you'd be a weakling, but you must have meat on those bones somewhere.' He coughed, a rattling cough, and spat on the ground. 'Couple more things, then we're done. Hop up there and you should find some sacks. Take 'em one at a time, cos they're heavy.'

I watched, my heart in my mouth, as Albert climbed up and then carefully down, holding a small sack and grimacing. 'What's in it? Weighs a ton!'

The gatekeeper laughed and then coughed again. 'Special stuff. Veeeeery important. Put it down carefully now.'

Albert went back for another sack, and another. 'That's it, then,' he said, setting it down.

'Not quite. Gotta get it into the factory, but I've got a trolley for that. You can 'elp load it.' He turned to the doors, and in the gap was a figure I recognised, even though he wore a linen mask over the lower part of his face.

Mr Sweet.

I looked for Albert, but he had withdrawn behind the wagon. I edged myself to the other side of the tree, and peeped out.

Mr Sweet pulled down the mask. 'Come here, Amos!' he shouted. His voice was clipped, with no trace of an accent.

'Wot, sir?' asked the gatekeeper, ambling over. 'Got a delivery to unload.'

'I can see that. But I have a more important delivery.' Mr Sweet reached behind him and handed Amos a large brown cardboard box. 'Get these into the river.'

Amos opened the lid and peered inside. 'What's wrong

with 'em? They seem all right to me.'

'The mix is wrong. Too strong. They've made the old recipe. Get them disposed of where no-one can see. Crush them; stamp on them. They cannot be found.'

'Right you are, sir.'

'Good. Get those sacks in, and then attend to this. The rest can wait.' Mr Sweet disappeared without waiting for an answer.

'Thanks for making yourself scarce, mate,' said Amos. 'I'd have been in bother if he'd caught yer. Like a sergeant-major, he is.' He coughed and spat again. 'And now all the way to the bloody river for these old bones, when I can barely walk to the gate.' He eyed Albert. 'Don't suppose you fancy another job?'

Albert tried to appear nonchalant. 'Wot, for another penny?'

'Yeah. I fancy a smoke, and I ain't allowed when I'm on duty, but I reckon I can say this job's a good twenty minutes.'

'You're on.'

'Put the sacks on the trolley then. I can't move 'em.' Amos wheeled the trolley through the double doors, closed and locked them, and handed Albert first two pennies, then the cardboard box. 'Now get yourself off. Make sure you do as 'e says, an' crush 'em, or my life won't be worth living. And you didn't see nuffink.'

'No,' said Albert. 'I didn't see nuffink.' And he hurried through the gate.

'Get them planks moved,' said the wagon driver. 'I've got a wife to go home to if you ain't. Ruddy Sunday deliveries, shouldn't be allowed.'

Amos kicked the planks aside, the wagon driver turned his horse, and a minute later they were trotting down the road. Amos watched them go, then locked the gates and strolled in the opposite direction from Albert.

'Oi!' I looked up. Reg, Dickie and Smudge were in the shadow of a closed-up building. 'Come on!' And we raced in the direction Albert had taken.

'Over here.' Albert was crouching in a doorway. He opened the flaps of the box and we saw the red, yellow and green of Crystal Kisses. 'Tredwell's waiting where we left him. Let's get these away.'

'Where to?' asked Smudge, as Albert closed the box. 'And 'ow d'you get them sweets? We couldn't get in the door!'

'Luck,' said Albert, rising and tucking the box under his arm. 'But I have a feeling this is a recipe which Mr Fraser doesn't know about. And whether he wants to know it or not, and whether it's a Sunday or not, we're going to tell him.'

CHAPTER 24
Katherine

'Oh Connie! I don't know whether to laugh or admonish!' I exclaimed. 'I hope you changed before you went to see Mr Fraser.' The image of her turning up in trousers and soot made me giggle. Laughing stopped me from worrying.

'Hahahaha!' agreed Ed and George with no idea what was happening. Ed had refused to be separated from me since waking the previous day, so here he was sitting with George on the office rug, scribbling on waste paper with coloured chalk while Connie and I caught up.

'Of course I changed,' said Connie with dignity. 'We looked very respectable when we arrived. Mr Fraser hadn't time to lose his temper. His wife was very calm and told him —' Connie wagged her finger as she quoted Mrs Fraser, '"Remember, Ernest: *for with what judgment ye judge, ye shall be judged* — Let them speak while I see

193

what Cook can rustle up.'" Connie grinned. 'Mrs Fraser was lovely. So were the cakes.'

I shook my head in wonder. 'When we met six years ago over stew, I never would have imagined you'd be the one doing this sort of thing. I'm quite jealous.'

'No you're not,' retorted Connie. She was as nervous as I as we waited for Mr Fraser. He had listened, but he had chosen to withhold his decision until this morning.

The sound of scribbling had changed and, looking over the edge of the desk, I realised the boys were inscribing loops and squiggles on the floorboards. At least it would wash off.

'But he seemed more reasonable?' I asked for the third time. If Mr Fraser arrived before Gwen and Lily, I could only hope the sight of two small children would keep him civil.

'To be honest,' said Connie, 'he seemed more deflated than angry. Rather like you on Saturday. As if all his dreams were crumbling… I'm sorry, I shouldn't have mentioned that.' Her already worried face became distressed.

'Don't worry,' I said. 'If anything, that description makes me feel better about whether we can trust Mr Fraser. I'll come to terms eventually with not having another baby, and so will James. But thank you for listening — and lending a cousin for Ed to play with.' We both glanced at the boys, jumped up to grab them before they started drawing on the walls, and held them at arms'-length to stop them getting chalk on our clothes. At this point, to our relief, Lily and Gwen arrived, heralded in by

Tina.

'Mamamama!' Ed wailed as I handed him over, reaching his dusty hands out.

'Mama will be home soon,' I promised. 'You're playing with George today.'

Ed's cries ceased and, with a sniff, he eyed George, who was grinning in Lily's arms and reaching out to hug him. 'Or?'

'George,' Connie corrected. 'All day.' I tried to ignore the nursemaids' careful expressions. It was hard to establish whether they were pleased or appalled. They'd have Nanny Kincaid to keep control, but they'd also have Bee teaching the boys new tricks. Ed pondered then grinned, giving me a large wet kiss and depositing a blue handprint on my white blouse before departing.

My heart ached a little, longing to spend more time with Ed, and at the same time I felt a tiny bit hurt that George was an acceptable substitute. I brushed the worst of the chalk from my shoulder and Connie made tea, her hands shaking a little. Mr Fraser was due any moment.

I checked myself in the mirror. 'I don't feel very professional any more,' I hoped Mr Fraser wouldn't notice the remaining blue smudge. At least it wasn't on my bosom.

'He'll be too busy reading these,' said Tina, hefting a basket onto Reg's desk and settling in his chair. To all intents and purposes it looked like shopping, but when she removed the checked cover she revealed a huge pile of letters each addressed to Mrs Minchin. 'I have to say underperforming husbands, uncontrollable urges and unwanted hair are less upsetting to read about. Until you asked, I hadn't realised how many there were. Usually someone helps me with the correspondence and weeds anything less than scandalous out.'

'The trouble is,' said Connie, picking up one of the letters, 'this is *real* scandal.'

'Yes it is,' said Tina. 'And I could barely sleep last night after reading them.'

There was a knock at the door, and I opened it to find Mr Fraser on the threshold. He fidgeted with the hat in his hands and I saw at once the expression Connie had described — as if something had crumbled to dust, and at the same time a simmering fury. I braced myself.

'Good morning, Mrs King and Mrs Lamont. May I enter?' He paused. 'I come begging forgiveness.'

'Of course.' I let him through, closed the door and went to my desk. Connie was sitting at hers, behind the tea-tray.

'My actions have been those of a man of pride rather than a man of peace,' Mr Fraser continued, waiting till I was seated before he himself sat down. 'I thought over your words, Mrs Lamont. I woke with the strong sense of things falling into place. Things I had ignored — or perhaps been led to ignore. This morning, early, I went to speak to Mr Sweet. He was not where I had expected him to be.'

Connie and I exchanged glances.

'I returned to the office and asked Mr Pearson for all the management staff particulars,' continued Mr Fraser. 'In doing so, I had the chance to look at Mr Sweet's file. It surprised me.'

He huffed a little and took the proffered teacup without drinking from it. I wondered if he was going to tell us that Mr Sweet's record was unblemished, but then I noticed Tina tensing, as if she was hearing unspoken words or unrounded thoughts.

Mr Fraser bit his lip. 'The file was empty. Or rather, it was full of blank paper. I said nothing to Mr Pearson about the file but asked if Mr Sweet might be at some *other place*.' He gave a mirthless chuckle. 'Mr Pearson seemed most incurious. All in all things don't add up, and I gave that sample of "old recipe" Crystal Kisses to the granddaughter of a friend to analyse. A Dr Naylor. The first thing she said was "Not these again", but then when she tasted one she promised a result this evening.'

He sighed. 'Ladies, I'd like to apologise once more for my shocking behaviour on Saturday. I should have asked you to explain before making assumptions.' His eyes drifted from my shoulder to the chalky floor and thence to the photographs on our desks. 'I can see that despite what I was given to understand by Mr Sweet, your families are very important to you and so, I gather, are your friends. I presume these are letters of support.' He indicated the basket.

'No,' said Tina. 'They're letters to an advice column asking for help with sickness, debilitation, anxiety and addiction connected with Crystal Kisses. Men, women, and children are affected. The children are from all classes, but otherwise the sweets lure young working adults. People like our friend Selina at the music hall, and Mrs King's housemaid Tamar.'

'I wish to meet them both immediately,' said Mr Fraser, rising, his tea still untouched. 'I feel there is no time to lose.'

***

His interview with Tamar was brief since she was prepared to say so little, and I made my mind up to talk to her later. She appeared not only shifty but frightened. Selina, however, was more than happy to give all the lurid details of her experience. If she expected Mr Fraser to be shocked by either her language, appearance or profession she was disappointed.

'I have never been to a music hall and doubt I ever shall,' he said. 'I enjoy music and jollity as much as the next person, but perhaps prefer it a little more — shall we say — discreet. However,' he glanced at me and Connie, 'perhaps I hadn't realised that the theatre can be a mirror on the world. Besides, no-one should be poisoned. I am old enough to remember all those cholera outbreaks and I've always believed that every man, woman and child deserves a pleasant life.'

He slammed his fist into his palm, his fury returned. 'I shall not have my endeavour, my vision ruined! Ladies — Miss Caster and Miss Fleet, I suppose I should call you — I give you my blessing and my help to find out everything you can. Now then, who can we trust? Ah yes! Mrs Guy.'

'Mrs Guy?' I asked.

'Yes. Mrs Lamont — Miss Fleet — will remember Mrs Guy. The mother of John who works in the factory and William who died.'

'Oh, yes,' said Connie. 'The grandmother.'

Mr Fraser nodded. 'It's only now her words to you sink in. "He went to train the other workers." I was so busy being proud, I wasn't listening. I remember William: he was in delicate health, but he was bright. I'd intended him to be given an apprenticeship as a clerk. We start a great many off that way. I used to follow them up — but I've been distracted for so many months. She's the one to see next.'

Mrs Guy greeted us at the door. She was feeding a baby with a bottle and pleased to welcome us in. She called to the back of the house, from which came childish giggles. 'Muriel — put the kettle on ducky. Mr Fraser's brung company.'

For an awful moment I thought she was instructing the toddler Connie had told me about, but then a cheery female voice called 'Yes Ma.' It sounded vaguely familiar.

'I'll leave the ladies here for ten minutes or so while I visit across the road,' said Mr Fraser. 'Don't be shy.' He donned his hat and left.

'This is nice,' said Mrs Guy. She scanned Connie from head to foot. 'I likes your dress Madam. Muriel will like it too. Blue's her favourite colour. Says it's cos it's the only colour they don't do sweets in!' She chuckled. 'Muriel's Mrs John. Remember, my daughter-in-law. She's just changed from morning to afternoon packing.'

'Of course,' said Connie. 'I remember. I wanted to say how sorry I was about your son William. When did he pass away?'

Mrs Guy's face fell a little. She nodded at a photograph on the mantel. 'Thought he'd go far. He wasn't strong from a child and his eyesight was poor, but he was bright as a new penny. Always asking how things worked, and why things were as they were. I used to tell him he was too clever for his own good. Mr Fraser said he'd make a clerk of him, but Mr Sweet said that'd waste his skills and sent him to train up the workers in the other factory instead, and make a new recipe.'

'The other factory?' I said, leaning forward.

'Ma! He told us never to say!' A shocked voice in the doorway made us turn. A young woman stood there with a tea-tray, a small child hiding behind her skirts. The woman's frightened gaze landed on me. It was the girl from the factory yard.

'Aren't you the one what was there for just one day?' she exclaimed. 'You look different. What are you doing here? Oh, thank the Lord you're all right!'

'Why wouldn't I be all right?' I said. 'I was only fired for being slow.'

'Then thank your stars you were,' Muriel said, putting the tea-tray down and pulling the toddler onto her hip. 'I thought you'd been sent to the other place for being nosy, same as William was.' She bit her lip as she realised what she'd said.

Mrs Guy started to demur and the baby grizzled as the bottle dropped from its mouth.

'You're right Ma, it's time to stop hiding things. We shoulda told someone a while ago. It's why they're here, ain't it? To find out. I shoulda known. William was too bright. He told us something wasn't right. Two weeks later he was dead.'

CHAPTER 25
Connie

'When did Allegra say she'd arrive?' asked Mr Fraser, for perhaps the tenth time that half-hour.

'At seven,' soothed his wife. 'You know how bad the traffic is.'

We were a motley company. Katherine and I had had no time to do more than snatch a quick sandwich and a cup of tea, much less change out of our day dresses, while Margaret was carefully dressed, as befitted someone about to mix socially with her lecturer. Albert was in his usual Savile Row tailoring, while James, who had been hanging around Greenland Dock all day in the role of a casual labourer looking for work, was dressed accordingly.

We watched the hand of the clock tick round. *Tempus fugit,* the dial warned; but not on this occasion.

'Here she is!' said Mrs Fraser brightly, as the doorbell clanged, and presently a small, dark woman, dressed rather rationally, was introduced as Dr Naylor. 'Do sit down, Allegra my dear. Would you like tea?'

'I'd like an explanation,' said Dr Naylor. 'What on earth has been going on at your factory, Mr Fraser?'

'Not at my factory!' blustered Mr Fraser. 'That's exactly the problem!'

'Indeed.' He squirmed under her cool gaze. 'I'm glad to hear it.' She surveyed us all, and I felt myself wilting slightly. 'I've analysed these sweets — or sweets like them — before, and found nothing worse than sugar and caffeine. These, however, are different.' She pulled a small glass jar from her pocket and gave it to James, who was nearest. 'Do you notice anything about this jar of sweets?'

James peered at it. 'I don't, but I'm not sure what I'm looking for.'

'Pass it on then, please.'

We each peered at the bright sweets in turn, but they seemed no different from any others we had seen. Margaret passed the jar to Mr Fraser, who exclaimed 'Why is the jar so heavy?'

'That's part of the problem,' said Dr Naylor. 'One ingredient, a sweet ingredient, is particularly heavy.'

'That must have been what was in the sacks I handled at Shaw and Sons,' said Albert. 'Those were as heavy as lead.'

'Top marks,' said Dr Naylor. 'My analysis of the sweets uncovered the usual sugar and caffeine, plus a significant proportion of sugar of lead. Sweet, heavy, poisonous, and potentially fatal. I doubt you use that for anything in your factory, Mr Fraser.'

'Certainly not,' snapped Mr Fraser.

'And that isn't all,' said Dr Naylor. 'The other ingredient which I certainly wouldn't expect to find in confectionery is cocaine. I was puzzled at first, since cocaine taken by mouth isn't absorbed particularly well. However, there is one way to increase its absorption and effectiveness.' She turned to Margaret. 'Miss Demeray, would you happen to know what it is?'

Margaret frowned. 'Could you mix it with an alkali?'

'Very good, Miss Demeray. The sharp lemon or lime-flavoured sweets contain just enough slaked lime to produce a much greater absorption rate.'

'Selina said the lemon and lime ones were her favourites!' I exclaimed. 'That's how she became so ill!'

'What would happen to someone who ate a quantity of these sweets, Dr Naylor?' asked Katherine.

'The effects vary.' Her small figure, even in a drawing room, was oddly impressive, and I wondered what it must be like to listen to her in a lecture theatre. 'In the short term, cocaine can bring about rapid heartbeat, increased energy and high temperature, and of course it is highly addictive. Over time this can shift to lethargy, insomnia, and paranoia.'

Katherine and I exchanged glances. 'What about the lead, Dr Naylor?' I asked.

'That's even more interesting. In adults I have seen joint pain, memory problems, headaches, and stomach pain. In children, however, the effect can be much more severe, starting with stomach pain and vomiting, through fatigue, to seizures and developmental problems.'

Katherine shivered. 'Tamar must have eaten sweets with lead in.'

Mr Fraser's fists clenched.

'Where did these come from?' Dr Naylor surveyed us all. 'The place must be shut down immediately.'

'They were meant to be destroyed,' I said. 'And yes, we are working to that end.'

Mr Fraser reached for the jar, held it close to his face, and rolled the sweets to and fro. The effect was of a child's kaleidoscope. 'These sweets would never be passed at my factory,' he said gruffly. 'They don't have the finish of a Fraser's sweet, and they aren't perfect spheres.'

'I doubt anyone cares about that at the other factory,' said Katherine. 'Plus I imagine it's useful to have sweets which aren't precisely identical. That would make it easier to mix a proportion of the two.'

'Do you think that's what they've been doing?' asked Albert.

Katherine nodded. 'Look at how many Selina ate before she collapsed. If she'd been eating these ones, she'd probably be dead. Hers must have had cocaine in, and her liking for the sour sweets made the effect worse. The tasters, though — that could be a different story. That would explain why Tamar was so ill after just one box.'

'I won't have it!' shouted Mr Fraser. 'These poor people! Poisoned by a business trading in my name!' His face crumpled. 'How are the mighty fallen,' he muttered.

'The thing I don't understand,' said Albert, 'is why.'

'Someone's trying to ruin me!' cried Mr Fraser. 'Isn't it obvious? And in my own firm!'

'But why? Why your firm, and not one of the other confectioners?' Albert's voice was reasonable. 'And Crystal Kisses have been very profitable.'

'I shall leave you to your business discussions,' said Dr Naylor, rising abruptly. 'If you don't mind.' She held out her hand for the jar. 'I expect to hear more about this very soon. If I do not, I shall be pursuing the matter with the appropriate authorities.' She put the jar into her pocket and swept out.

'Isn't she wonderful?' said Margaret, once the front door had closed.

'She's terrifying,' said Mr Fraser, with feeling.

'She's right,' I said. 'What now?'

'We use the weapons at our disposal,' said Albert. 'May I use your telephone?'

'What will you do?' I asked. 'We don't have long. Tina's column will appear on Wednesday, and all hell will break loose.'

'*We*,' said Albert, 'shall conduct an audit.'

***

'Ready?' asked Albert, gripping the handle of his briefcase tightly.

'Ready,' replied Mr Anstruther, doing likewise.

They marched up to the gates of Fraser's, Katherine and I well in the rear.

'We're here to see Mr Fraser,' Albert told the gatekeeper. 'He is expecting us.'

'Indeed I am!' shouted Mr Fraser from the entrance. 'Come in, come in.'

'So far so good,' muttered Katherine.

Mr Pearson met us at the office door. 'This isn't a good time for visitors, Mr Fraser,' he said reproachfully. 'You know that the morning is when we are busiest.'

'Never mind all that,' said Mr Fraser. 'These gentlemen have come to audit our accounts, and not before time.'

Mr Pearson's face froze for a split second. 'Under whose authority?' he asked.

'Mine,' said Mr Fraser.

Work had completely stopped in the office as all the clerks watched the scene, pens in mid-air, pages mid-turn.

A weak smile spread across Mr Pearson's face. 'I'm afraid I can't let that happen,' he said, trying to back us towards the door.

'Really?' asked Albert, not budging. 'Whose orders are you following?'

'Those of the controlling stakeholder,' said Mr Pearson, smugly. 'I must ask you to leave.'

'And I must ask you to let the gentlemen proceed,' said a gruff voice from the doorway. Chief Inspector Barnes removed his hat and walked into the room. 'I have authority to enter and search these premises, in case you were wondering. I strongly suggest you cooperate, Mr Pearson.'

'I'll just go into my office,' gabbled Mr Pearson.

'No you won't,' said the Chief Inspector. 'The gentlemen will be using it. And your telephone, if necessary. You, Mr Pearson, will sit down where I can see you, and stay there.'

***

'It's taking a long time,' said Katherine, fidgeting on

her chair.

We were all fidgeting. The clerks had been told to stop work and huddled in groups, talking quietly, eyeing the closed door of Mr Pearson's office. Albert, Mr Anstruther, and Mr Fraser were closeted inside. Every so often the buzzer would sound and a clerk would answer the summons, then scurry out to fetch another box or ledger. Meanwhile Mr Pearson twitched on a clerk's high stool under the watchful eye of the Chief Inspector. He had been asked for the combination of the safe early in the proceedings, and after some prevarication had given it. Thereafter his face wore the expression of a condemned man.

The door swung open. 'You scoundrel, Pearson!' barked Mr Fraser. 'You, a man I trusted, to misrepresent my own business to me!'

Mr Pearson nearly fell off his stool. 'Mr Fraser, I can explain —'

'I'm sure you can. I'm sure you could tie me up in ledger talk like a kipper. But now I've seen it all. I've seen what's in the safe which you could never find the combination to, every time I asked. My best lines damned as unprofitable and discontinued! Profits shown as losses! All to bring in a rescuer whose mission was to expose me to shame and ridicule, if not worse!' He paused for breath. 'And to think, Samuel, that your father was my good friend.' He shook his head.

'Is there enough evidence to arrest him?' asked the Chief Inspector.

Albert, grave-faced, appeared beside Mr Fraser. 'Oh

yes.'

'Excellent,' said Chief Inspector Barnes, and pulled a set of handcuffs from his pocket.

***

'MUPR,' Albert spelt out. 'I have no idea what that stands for.'

Albert and Mr Anstruther had extracted the holding company papers from the safe, and we pored over them together.

'Raponia,' said Mr Anstruther.

'I beg your pardon?' Katherine and I said in unison.

'It's a tiny principality in eastern Europe. Tiny, but disproportionately powerful for two reasons; it is ridiculously rich in oil, and it controls the Dardanelles, an extremely important trade route.' He held up one of the thick, heavy sheets of paper on which the agreement was typed. 'See.' The paper was watermarked with a crest showing a three-headed lion. 'That's on the Raponian flag. I've seen MUPR before, too. Manufacturing Union of the Principality of Raponia.'

Mr Fraser frowned. 'What on earth would a tinpot place like Raponia want with my factory? Why would bags of sweets in Britain matter to them?'

'Good question,' said Albert. 'Numbers I can understand, but this is beyond me.'

'Wait a moment...' mused Katherine. 'Hasn't Raponia been in the newspaper lately?'

'Oh yes,' I said. 'Something about rumblings? Wanting to form a federation of countries.'

'That's it,' said Albert. 'It sounded like empire-building.'

'Mmm,' said Mr Anstruther, looking worried. 'Their Crown Prince is a loose cannon, and has been ever since he seized power five years ago.'

I drew a sheet of paper and a pencil towards me. 'So a power-hungry little country, taking over a reputable British confectioner, to feed the population poisoned sweets —' My mouth fell open.

'Not the whole population,' said Katherine. 'They're targeting young people and children.' Her face had lost all its colour.

'And if in a few years this federation declared war on Britain, what sort of fighting force would we have? We wouldn't be able to stop them,' I whispered. 'Their plan is to weaken the Empire.'

'There was something in the *Times* this morning,' said Mr Anstruther. 'I only had time to glance at it, though.'

'I have a copy delivered,' said Mr Fraser. 'I read it when it's quiet, or I'm not allowed in the office.' His tone was bitter. 'Wait here a moment.'

He was back in a few minutes, the folded paper in his hand. 'Here.'

We spread the newspaper on Mr Pearson's desk, scanning the pages for a mention of Raponia. 'Here,' said Mr Anstruther, stabbing a finger. 'Page five.'

RAPONIA RESTRICTS SHIPPING THROUGH DARDANELLES, I read. *Exports threatened.* Beneath the headline was a small photograph of a slender, neatly-bearded man, labelled *Crown Prince Ferdinand of Raponia*.

I gasped, and struggled to speak, but Mr Fraser was before me. 'That's a very familiar face,' he breathed. 'Not exactly like, but definitely related.'

'The Crown Prince has a younger brother, Armand,' said Mr Anstruther. 'He is a minister for industry in the country.'

'Not right now he isn't,' I said, touching the newspaper. 'He's Mr Sweet.'

Chapter 26
Katherine

When we left Fraser's, it was raining again.

Tredwell drove us as briskly as the traffic would allow. Inspector Barnes had declared that we should all convene in an hour at Shaw and Sons to apprehend Mr Sweet.

'Do you think anyone was watching?' I said, as we rushed down the main road.

'I don't think so,' answered Connie. 'It's hard to make anyone out in this drizzle. At least Chief Inspector Barnes had all his men come in plain clothes.'

'I never thought I'd be glad to see rain.' I checked my watch. It was ten a.m. 'The clerks' lunch break is at one o'clock,' I said. 'No-one will notice they've been locked in until then. Three hours. That's all the time we have. We must fetch James and say goodbye to the children.'

'Never goodbye,' said Connie, her face white but her eyes flashing. 'Au revoir.'

I was dropped off first and scurried up the steps, latchkey at the ready, to find the front door wrenched open by Margaret. A hideous shrieking and wailing could be heard coming from the direction of the kitchen. My heart jumped into my mouth.

'Thank God you're here,' said Margaret. 'I was just going for a bobby.'

'Have they —?'

'Tamar's young man tried to abduct her. I want him arrested before Ada clubs him to death. Oh good — there's a constable on the other side of the park.' Putting her fingers between her lips, she let out a piercing whistle and beckoned when he turned. Several passing ladies eyed us both with utter disgust. Margaret blew them a kiss and pushed me inside. 'I'll deal with this. You're on a mission, I can tell.'

'Where's Ed? You said you'd look after him while Gwen had the morning off.'

'He's in the kitchen with Susan,' she said, and beckoned to the policeman to hurry with such authority that he broke into a run.

Why was Ed being allowed to witness whatever was happening? And why did it have to happen now? I ran down the hall and burst into the kitchen. Utter pandemonium met me. Tamar was wailing while her young man, tied to a chair with a length of washing line, was struggling and shouting at Ada. She was whacking him with a tea-towel in one hand and threatening him with a rolling-pin in the other.

Ed, wriggling in Susan's arms, crowed with delight.

'Mamamama, Bissit bash!'

Susan saw me and gabbled without taking a breath, 'Oh ma'am it all happened so fast I haven't had time to take Master Ed out!'

'Mamamama, Bissit bash! Maggot bash!' said Ed.

'Get this flaming dragon off me!' shouted Tamar's young man.

'You tried to drag Tamar away,' cried Ada. 'I saw you.'

''S'all lies,' said the man, his beady little eyes looking everywhere for a way out. Like a cornered rat.

'You said you wanted to shut my mouth for good!' wailed Tamar. 'Just cos I told you someone came asking questions! An' I never said anything! An' what was in them sweets, anyway?'

The man squirmed and hissed. 'Shut it, or so help me I'll —'

I gasped and turned to Margaret, coming in with the constable. I whispered in her ear and her eyes widened.

'I see,' she said. 'Leave it with me. Do whatever you have to do. I'm in charge here.' She cracked her knuckles, grinned, then gave me a quick kiss. 'Be careful. You may be small and bossy, but you're the only sister I've got.'

***

'That horrible man is squeaking to the police,' I said to Connie as the cab rushed towards Southwark. 'Tamar was inconsolable until she realised he didn't care if she died. Then she took over from Ada and had to be dragged off him.'

'So he was the person behind the samples?'

'It appears so. Margaret will make sure the constable

gets word to Chief Inspector Barnes.'

The roads became narrow and more rutted, puddles deeper than they appeared. Wharves and warehouses loomed and wiry, grubby men paused in their work to watch us pass. Shaggy-headed children lurked everywhere and yet they all seemed too listless to keep out of the rain.

We waited in an alley near Shaw and Sons. Reg emerged from a doorway and, as if we were strangers, asked for a light. James offered a match.

Reg took a drag of his cigarette and coughed. 'The geezer who brings the cards from the PO box address was late. Someone was out looking for him. I accidentally found myself walking past and I heard him say, "Today's samples haven't gone out". He wasn't too happy.'

'I'll bet,' I said.

'Ah,' said Connie. 'Here's Mr Fraser in a brougham, and the Chief Inspector with his men in a carriage.'

'We can get started, then,' said Reg, rubbing his hands.

Our small group, with Mr Fraser at the front, knocked on the main door. When it opened one of the larger policemen planted his foot firmly across the threshold to ensure it couldn't be closed. The man on the other side stammered 'W-what — h-how can I help you?'

'Factory inspection,' said Chief Inspector Barnes. 'We'd like to speak to the man in charge while my men check on conditions. And ingredients.'

As they headed for the factory and storerooms, the man turned a sickly shade of green, reminiscent of the poisoned sweets, and called hoarsely for Mr Hynes.

'It's Sweet we want,' snapped Mr Fraser. 'Who's

Hynes?'

The doorman didn't answer but simply shouted again, this time louder and with more confidence, 'Mr Hynes!'

Somewhere an alarm started to clang.

'What's that?' The Chief Inspector grabbed the man by his collar and hauled him half off his feet.

'One of your men must be interfering,' whined the man. 'We're very particular here.'

'Let's see how particular, shall we?' snarled the Chief Inspector, frog-marching the doorman forward. 'Mr Hynes can catch up with us in the factory. You —' He grabbed a worker who was trying to edge away. 'Go with Constable Parker and get Mr Sweet.'

'B-b-but the alarm's sounding.'

'Really? I can't hear anything.' Constable Parker chivvied the worker forward while we entered the factory, putting masks on before we did so. Above us a gallery ran round the edges of the building, and small sacks and crates filled with sample boxes were piled around us. We could see through the grid-like floor to the upper level and in the centre fumes rose from huge boiling vats of luminescent coloured sugar. Vapour glowed in many colours against the grey sky visible through the high windows.

Men in aprons and heavy boots, more listless than the children outside, stood poised with stirring poles and metal scoops as policemen prodded and pried. If the alarm worried them, they looked as if the effort required to run would be too much to bear. One of them scooped some powder out of a sack, but missed the vat and the powder fell on the floor, rising in a white cloud. The man coughed, then clutched his stomach and staggered away.

Albert grabbed his arm. 'Where's the foreman here?' Someone who appeared healthier, without an apron, stepped forward. 'Where's Mr Sweet?'

The foreman shrugged but the sweat on his brow ran more freely.

'Who's Mr Hynes?'

The man Albert was restraining giggled. 'It's the man what made the alarm. Hynes is the name embossed on it.' He groaned.

'Lead powder in the storeroom,' confirmed one of the constables.

'Safe's open in the office,' said Constable Parker, returning with the squirming doorman. 'Sweet's scarpered, but he left this behind.' He held up a letter in a foreign language, a now-familiar crest printed at the top. 'Not that I know what it says.'

James took it. 'I know a few words of Raponian. This is beyond me but I can guess at "well done" and "Crown Prince Ferdinand" and "brother". It's probably all you need.' He handed it to the Chief Inspector. 'As long as your men have captured him.'

'Right,' said Chief Inspector Barnes, turning to the workers. 'You lot, stay here. And put the furnaces out while you're waiting to be taken to the infirmary. I'll work out what to do with you later.' The factory hands collapsed against the walls. One of them started to weep. It seemed to be more from relief than fear.

But as we marched out of the building a sergeant rushed towards us, his face grim.

'It's no good, sir. Sweet got out of a window. Grange nearly apprehended him but got shot at close range. We're trying to save him. Sweet's legged it on a worker's bicycle. He was round the corner before I could say knife and he could have gone any which way after that. I've sent two of the lads to Butler's Wharf. There's a ship about to sail.'

'I'll follow them,' said Mr Fraser. 'I'll recognise him.'

'He could have gone to the cathedral hoping for sanctuary,' said Albert. 'Someone can go there.'

'You two, head for the cathedral,' Chief Inspector Barnes ordered his men. 'And the rest of you go to Borough Market. He'll be hoping to get lost in the crowd.' Within seconds, they had all departed.

'Wait…' said James, frowning. 'Wouldn't he head for the Raponian embassy?'

'Where is it?' asked Connie.

'Tower Hill,' said Albert. 'Five minutes by bicycle. All he has to do is cross Tower Bridge and turn left.'

I looked round. Mr Fraser's brougham was nearby. 'We could borrow that, couldn't we?'

'Of course,' Connie agreed. 'But we mustn't take risks. The man is armed. All we have to do is stop him getting inside. Won't he be on his own soil then?'

'I'm not sure,' said James. 'It depends on treaties, but at any rate, Sweet might think so.'

'We have to try,' I said, clambering into the cramped brougham.

James clicked and the horse set off at a good speed. His hunch was right. Even in the rain we could make out Mr Sweet by the haphazard way he zigzagged in and out of the traffic as he sped across the bridge.

'We must catch him quickly,' shouted Connie. 'If only this horse could go faster or this wretched traffic would…' She leaned out of the carriage. 'Stop that bicyclist!' she cried, pointing.

But no-one heard in the commotion. The bridge was not just busy with vehicles but pedestrians too, marvelling at the structure as if it were not already two years old, stepping in front of omnibuses and cabs as if they were invincible and causing near-collisions.

Ahead of us Mr Sweet cycled off the bridge and turned left past the Tower of London, and we followed.

'There's the embassy!' shouted Albert.

A grand building resplendent with a flag bearing the Raponian crest was yards away. If we didn't hurry, Mr Sweet — or rather Prince Armand — would be inside and under the protection of his own country. Just as it seemed impossible we could get to him in time, a small figure stepped off the pavement, waving. Mr Sweet lost his balance and fell into the gutter.

'I know that girl!' I said as we neared. 'That's Linnie from the Merrymakers!'

'Armand!' she cried. 'Where you going? I was coming to meet you like you said.'

The brougham came to a halt and we jumped out.

'Stop right there!' shouted James. Both figures turned. Linnie was pulling at Mr Sweet and he was shaking her off, making for the embassy steps.

'Leave me alone, you stupid woman,' he snarled, unpeeling her clasping hands only to have her paw at him again. 'I'm going home.'

'Take me too,' Linnie wailed.

'Don't be such a fool,' he snapped.

'But you said you'd take me with you! You said you loved me!'

'You? A dancing girl?' He pushed her hard and she staggered into my arms. James, Albert, Connie and I closed in, but Mr Sweet drew his revolver and pointed it in our direction.

'Don't think you can capture me,' he snarled. 'I have enough bullets for each of you and I never miss.' He started to back away, and with sinking hearts we watched as the doors of the embassy opened and three armed soldiers emerged onto the steps.

Mr Sweet smiled, but his voice was cold with fury. 'You think you've won, but you wait. My country will soon be greater than yours and when it is, I'll hunt you four down and wipe you out. You *and* your families. Your people are weak — rushing brainlessly for the next new thing, never thinking for themselves, believing anything — easy to fool like that creature there.' He nodded at the weeping dancer. 'Raponia will prevail! And *I* shall be in control!' He moved backwards up the steps towards his soldiers. We could do nothing. Four guns were pointed at us.

Then the soldiers cocked their rifles, and fired.

Mr Sweet — Prince Armand — fell on the threshold of the embassy. He twitched for a few moments, his hands clutching at his wounds as if he could stem the blood draining his life away. Then he choked and his head lolled, eyes staring at nothing.

Linnie broke from my arms and fell to cradle his body. 'He promised I'd be a princess,' she cried. 'He promised!'

A tall imperious figure stepped through the soldiers.

'Clear that mess up,' he ordered. 'It's bringing shame on our glorious new country. The time for princes is over. Long live the Republic of Raponia!'

CHAPTER 27
Connie

'Are you sure I look all right?' asked Katherine, adjusting her hat for the fiftieth time.

'You look lovely,' I said, patting her carefully so as not to disturb her leg-o-mutton sleeve. 'Will I do?'

'Of course.' Katherine grinned. 'Although you were more impressive as Britannia.'

'Don't remind me.' I snorted. 'Perhaps not quite the thing for today, though.'

'No,' Katherine mused. 'It's rather too warm.'

***

On the morning after the end of the case I had waited impatiently for the papers to be delivered. I had ordered an extra copy of the *Messenger* specially, so that we would have a record of Tina's column for our files. But when Johnson brought the papers into the breakfast room he had an uncharacteristic grin on his face. 'I think you ought to see this, ma'am,' he said, laying the *Messenger* in front of me.

I goggled.

CASTER AND FLEET CRACK THE CASE!, the headline shouted.

Our heroines pursue crazed foreign prince across Tower Bridge.

EMPIRE SAVED BY TWO PLUCKY WOMEN.

'But it wasn't just us,' I said, dazed.

Albert came over and, leaning down, put his arm round me. 'I think you and K have caught the public imagination.'

'Oh dear.' I pushed the *Messenger* aside and found the *Times*, which was much more sensible on the matter. But my perusal of their piece was disturbed by a chuckle.

'What is it?' I asked, lowering the paper to see Albert wiping away a tear.

'It's — ah — you'll have to see for yourself.' And he pushed the *London Daily News* across the table.

It was a cartoon. I was dressed as Britannia, and Katherine, similarly robed, was standing on the top edge of our chariot, which appeared to have swords attached to the wheels. In front of us were a mass of villainous-looking people, fleeing from our rearing horses. The caption read *Giddy-up, Pegasus, or we'll miss afternoon tea!*

'Gosh.' That was all I could manage. 'I'm going to telephone Katherine,' I said, getting up.

The telephone shrilled before I was even out of the room. 'Have you seen it?' Katherine cried.

'How could I miss it?' I replied. 'But —'

'I know.' She paused. 'We're probably the most recognisable undercover detectives in England right now.'

'Maybe it'll blow over,' I said.

'And maybe things will be different.'

I couldn't make out Katherine's tone. 'Different in a good way?' I asked, trying to keep the hope out of my voice.

Katherine paused. '*Yes*,' she said, decisively. 'Let's *make* it different in a good way.'

The doorbell rang, and Johnson bustled past, puffed-up, to answer it.

On the doorstep stood Reg, holding a bunch of tulips.

'Oh, um, good morning Reg,' I said, taken aback. 'That's very kind of you.'

'Is Lily in, Miss F?' he asked, running a finger round his stiff collar.

'Er, yes, she will be in the nursery —'

'Good.' And he ran upstairs.

'What's going on?' Katherine demanded.

'Reg is here. With flowers. To see Lily.'

'Why are you still on the line, Connie? Go and find out what's happening!'

'I'll call you back,' I said, handed the receiver to Johnson, and set off upstairs in pursuit.

I entered the nursery to find Reg on one knee, Lily all smiles and blushes, Bee jumping up and down like a mad thing, and George pulling gently on Reg's sleeve, asking if he wanted to play 'sojers'.

'I take it all is well,' I said, and the party turned to me.

Reg got up, and kissed Lily's hand. 'I learnt something

yesterday, Miss F,' he said. 'Anyone could've died when that maniac was shooting. You got to take your chances while you can. I swore then that if I got out alive, this was the first thing I'd do. Well, after a good night's sleep, but you know what I mean.'

Lily threw her arms around Reg. Nanny Kincaid, coming in with a pile of towels, gave her a disapproving look which became a shy smile when she saw I was doing nothing to stop it.

'I'll, um, see myself out,' I said, and withdrew.

'So what happened?' Katherine asked.

'Reg and Lily are getting married,' I said, in a daze.

'Oh yes, I thought that would be it,' she said.

'Reg has grown up.'

'Um, yes,' she said, laughing. Then a pause. 'I see what you mean. I think we all have. I'll come over in a bit. Once Ed has had his breakfast, and we've had a play.'

'That would be lovely. I'll see you soon, Katherine.'

Albert was still breakfasting, deep in our exploits as recounted by all the newspapers. I leaned down to kiss him.

'Mmm. What's that for?'

'Just because.' I kissed him again. 'And because Reg is a very intelligent young man.'

'That he is,' said Albert, pulling me onto his lap. 'Particularly if he recommends this sort of behaviour at the breakfast table.' And for a few minutes all thought of the future was forgotten.

***

The freshly-created Republic of Raponia disclaimed all

responsibility for Prince Armand's actions, blaming them on 'the diseased system of hereditary rule'. The deposed Crown Prince Ferdinand, now living quietly in exile, professed ignorance of the whole affair. And as the killing of Prince Armand, once Mr Sweet, had taken place in the Raponian embassy (and thus, some might argue, on Raponian soil), that was that. At any rate, no prosecutions were possible since the soldiers had conveniently disappeared.

Mr Fraser took a full-page advertisement in every newspaper to apologise to the British people, and assure them that such a thing would never happen again. The profits from Crystal Kisses were devoted to the care of the workers at Shaw and Sons, and that factory was razed to the ground, and the equipment destroyed.

'And now what?' Mr Fraser asked, gazing dejectedly into the flames of the drawing-room fire while Mrs Fraser managed the teapot and handed cups.

'How d'you mean, Mr Fraser?' asked Albert.

'The business needs to be built back up. Old favourites reintroduced, and new sweets and chocolates brought in. Otherwise Fry and Cadbury will finish me off. It's a dog-eat-dog world in confectionery.' He sighed. 'I'm not getting any younger, and I'm not sure I have the energy.'

'What about your nephew?' I asked.

'Him?' Mr Fraser looked ready to spit. 'He wants nothing more to do with the business — except to inherit it after I'm gone. No, I need someone with a business brain who knows sweets — properly knows 'em.'

'Would I do?' asked Albert. 'I may not have a

background in making sweets, but I've a lifetime's experience in eating them.'

Mr Fraser gave Albert an appraising glance. 'All right, answer me this. What would you do first?'

Albert stretched out his long legs and drained his cup. 'Well,' he said, setting it down, 'why not make sweets that really are good for you? Not packed full of caffeine, but with, um, vitamins and other things. Sort of fortified. Dr Naylor could probably advise you.'

Mr Fraser slapped his knee. 'So she could! Genius, my man, genius!'

And so Albert swapped his study for Fraser's factory two days a week. Bee came running when she heard him come home, to see what treats he might have in his brown-paper bag of samples. And on those days he was, as he put it, as happy as a kid in a sweetshop.

***

'Come along,' I said. 'We'll be late.'

Katherine sighed and pushed a hairpin out of sight. 'All right.'

We left the beautifully-appointed bathroom. 'If you would be so kind as to follow me,' said the wigged and powdered footman, and we fell into step behind him.

'At least you've met her before,' muttered Katherine. 'No wonder you're so calm.'

'I was eighteen,' I murmured back. 'And it was for about thirty seconds. I was so busy making sure I didn't fall over my own feet that I don't remember a thing.'

'Don't make that mistake again.'

'What, falling over my own feet?'

'No, the other one,' Katherine whispered fiercely.

The corridor seemed to go on for ever. 'I know what I meant to ask you,' I said. 'Whatever happened to James's novel? The one about . . . what was it about?'

Katherine let out a tiny snort. 'I asked him that the other day. He said he'll put that one down to experience and write detective stories instead. He's working on one now. I read a bit and, to be fair, it wasn't any less unbelievable than the sort of thing that happens to us.' She giggled. 'He said we have to keep the agency going for plot ideas.'

'Oh honestly.'

We were approaching two gilded double doors. They opened as if by magic when we were a few steps away.

The letter, when it came, had surprised and horrified me, so much so that I had telephoned Mother who had, to my astonishment, waited patiently while I poured out my bewilderment and anxiety.

'Have you finished?' she asked, when I finally came to a stop.

I nodded, then realised she couldn't see me. 'Yes, Mother.'

'Good. Of course you should accept it.'

'But it wasn't just us, there were lots of people involved and —'

'And you kept going when most women — most *people* — would have run away with their tails between their legs. You deserve it, Connie, and you must accept it, as a good example to women everywhere.' I thought I heard a sniffle on the other end of the line, but I must have been mistaken. 'And you *have* to accept it, so that I can show the announcement in the *London Gazette* to all my friends. There.'

I felt as small as an ant as we proceeded through the stateroom, where a long line of people stood ready. The line was in order of rank, with the highest honours on the right-hand side as we approached.

A steward holding a list advanced to meet us. 'Mrs King and Mrs Lamont? Very good. Royal Victorian Medal, Gold . . . your place is here.' He indicated a small gap between a pair of uncomfortable-looking men, and we squeezed into it.

'Are you Caster and Fleet?' whispered the man on my right-hand side.

'We are,' I whispered back.

'Jolly good show,' he said, facing the front again.

A trumpet fanfare made me jump, and I felt Katherine's hand slip into mine. I glanced down, and she smiled up at me. 'Don't worry about your feet,' she said.

'I won't. And you still look lovely.'

I shall have so much to tell them afterwards, I thought, as a tiny, black-clad, crowned figure advanced down the red carpet towards us. Everyone would be waiting for us in the palace grounds: Albert and James and the children, my family and Katherine's; not to mention Reg and Tina. But for now I revelled in the thought that Katherine and I, two women who had climbed out of windows, dressed up as men, pranced around on a stage and generally indulged in all sorts of unladylike behaviour, were thoroughly approved of by Her Majesty, Queen Victoria.

Acknowledgements

As ever, our first thanks go to our beta readers — Ruth Cunliffe, Christine Downes, Stephen Lenhardt, and Val Portelli. Many, many thanks for sticking with us throughout the series! Even bigger thanks than usual are due to John Croall, whose chemical expertise saved us from a scientific slip-up just in time, along with his meticulous proofreading. Any errors remaining in the book are of course the responsibility of the authors.

As well as our usual diving into Wikipedia, The Victorian Web, (http://www.victorianweb.org) and Victorian London (http://www.victorianlondon.org/index-2012.htm), we'd like to cite a few other sources:

Our Baby: For Mothers and Nurses by J. Langton-Hewer, first published 1891 and reprinted many times.

An article from the Mayo Clinic on lead poisoning: https://www.mayoclinic.org/diseases-conditions/lead-poisoning/symptoms-causes/syc-20354717.

'The Inexorable Rise of Synthetic Flavor: A Pictorial

History', by Nadia Berenstein: https://www.popsci.com/history-flavors-us-pictorial.

And a great big thank-you to you, our reader! We've had a blast writing the Caster & Fleet series, and it's great to know that so many readers have come along for the ride. We hope you've enjoyed Katherine and Connie's latest, and for now last, adventure, and if you could leave the book a short review — or a star rating — on Amazon or Goodreads we'd be very grateful.

Font and image credits

Fonts:

Main cover font: Birmingham Titling by Paul Lloyd (freeware):
https://www.fontzillion.com/fonts/paul-lloyd/birmingham.

Classic font: Libre Baskerville Italic by Impallari Type (http://www.impallari.com): https://www.fontsquirrel.com/fonts/libre-baskerville License — SIL Open Font License v.1.10: http://scripts.sil.org/OFL

Graphics:

Scales (decolourised and cropped): Balance scale by Henry N. Hooper and Co, part of the collection of the Metropolitan Museum of Art: https://www.metmuseum.org/art/collection/search/629597. Open access: public domain.

Sweets (cropped, decolourised and coloured): Marbles/

Murmein IV by Christian Schnettelke (https://www.manoftaste.de) at https://www.flickr.com/photos/manoftaste-de/15184832866. License: Creative Commons license 2.0 — https://creativecommons.org/licenses/by/2.0/.

The photographs of the chess pieces are the cover designer's own and not to be reproduced without permission.

Cover created using GIMP image editor: www.gimp.org.

About Paula Harmon

At her first job interview, Paula Harmon answered the question 'where do you see yourself in 10 years' with 'writing', as opposed to 'progressing in your company.' She didn't get that job. She tried teaching and realised the one thing the world did not need was another bad teacher. Somehow or other she subsequently ended up as a civil servant and if you need to know a form number, she is your woman.

Her short stories include dragons, angst ridden teenagers, portals and civil servants (though not all in the same story — yet). Perhaps all the life experience was worth it in the end.

Paula is a Chichester University English graduate. She is married with two children and lives in Dorset. She is currently working on a thriller, a humorous murder mystery and something set in an alternative universe. She's wondering where the housework fairies are, because the house is a mess and she can't think why.

Website: www.paulaharmondownes.wordpress.com
Amazon author page: http://viewAuthor.at/PHAuthorpage
Goodreads: https://goodreads.com/paula_harmon
Twitter: https://twitter.com/PaulaHarmon789

Books by Paula Harmon

Murder Britannica
When Lucretia's plan to become very rich is interrupted by a series of unexpected deaths, local wise-woman Tryssa starts to ask questions.

Murder Durnovaria (Spring 2020)
An ancient grove, broken promises, a lost keepsake: who cares about the old bones two hapless grave robbers unearth? How can Tryssa find out who would rather kill than reveal the truth?

The Cluttering Discombobulator
Can everything be fixed with duct tape? Dad thinks so. The story of one man's battle against common sense and the family caught up in the chaos around him.

Kindling
Is everything quite how it seems? Secrets and mysteries, strangers and friends. Stories as varied and changing as British skies.

The Advent Calendar
Christmas as it really is, not the way the hype says it is (and sometimes how it might be) — stories for midwinter.

The Quest
In a parallel universe, dragons are used for fuel and the

people who understand them are feared as spies and traitors. Can two estranged sisters, descended from the dragon-people, save the country from revolution?

Weird and Peculiar Tales (with Val Portelli)
Short stories from this world and beyond.

About Liz Hedgecock

Liz Hedgecock grew up in London, England, did an English degree, and then took forever to start writing. After several years working in the National Health Service, some short stories crept into the world. A few even won prizes. Then the stories began to grow longer . . .

Now Liz travels between the nineteenth and twenty-first centuries, murdering people. To be fair, she does usually clean up after herself.

Liz's reimaginings of Sherlock Holmes, her Pippa Parker cozy mystery series, and *Bitesize*, a collection of flash fiction, are available in ebook and paperback.

Liz lives in Cheshire with her husband and two sons, and when she's not writing or child-wrangling you can usually find her reading, messing about on Twitter, or cooing over stuff in museums and art galleries. That's her story, anyway, and she's sticking to it.

Website/blog: http://lizhedgecock.wordpress.com
Facebook: http://www.facebook.com/lizhedgecockwrites
Twitter: http://twitter.com/lizhedgecock
Goodreads: https://www.goodreads.com/lizhedgecock

Books by Liz Hedgecock

Short stories
The Secret Notebook of Sherlock Holmes
Bitesize

Halloween Sherlock series (novelettes)
The Case of the Snow-White Lady
Sherlock Holmes and the Deathly Fog
The Case of the Curious Cabinet

Sherlock & Jack series (novellas)
A Jar Of Thursday
Something Blue
A Phoenix Rises

Mrs Hudson & Sherlock Holmes series (novels)
A House Of Mirrors
In Sherlock's Shadow

Pippa Parker Mysteries (novels)
Murder At The Playgroup
Murder In The Choir
A Fete Worse Than Death
Murder In The Meadow
The QWERTY Murders (winter 2019)

Caster & Fleet Mysteries (with Paula Harmon)
The Case of the Black Tulips
The Case of the Runaway Client
The Case of the Deceased Clerk

The Case of the Masquerade Mob
The Case of the Fateful Legacy
The Case of the Crystal Kisses

Printed in Great Britain
by Amazon